93x 11/10 √12/11
94x 8/12 √12/12

VA

VA

S0-DTA-752

"Now, listen!" says Nancy. "I don't mind your playing in the bathroom, but *only* in the bathroom!"

All the animals sigh with relief.

"And you must ALWAYS wipe your feet!" Some animals look very guilty.

"You can wipe them on the bath mat when you first come out of the painting!"

The animals are happy. They do as she asks.

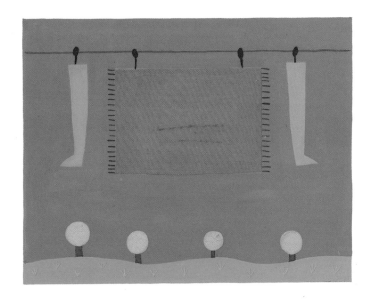

Nancy is very happy. She has a new painting to look at every day because the animals never remember *exactly* where they were.

And Nancy always remembers to clean the bath mat very, very carefully before she hangs it outside. If she didn't, she would have a lot to explain to her neighbors at the bus stop.

afraid to move
a feather or a furry foot.

Another story for Jane,
somewhere in America.

CIP Data is available.

First published in the United States 1993 by Dutton Children's Books,
a division of Penguin Books USA Inc.
375 Hudson Street, New York, New York 10014

Originally published as *Mysterious Footprints* in Great Britain 1992
by ABC, All Books for Children,
a division of The All Children's Company Ltd., London

Printed in Hong Kong   First American Edition
10 9 8 7 6 5 4 3 2 1   ISBN 0-525-44992-2

Wipe Your Feet!

by

Daniel Lehan

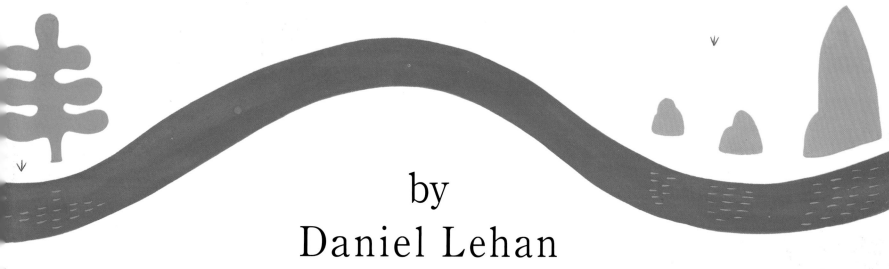

Dutton Children's Books

New York

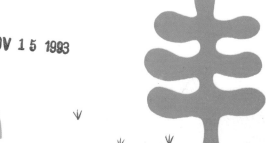

Birds are singing as Nancy Moore leaves her house.

It is Thursday, and every
Thursday there is a yard sale
at the Town Hall. Nancy always
buys something—a scarf, a clock.
Once, she even bought a big
blue chair.

Today she finds a painting
of wild animals who seem to
be happy. This makes Nancy
happy, too, so she buys the
painting and takes it home.

First she puts it at the top of the stairs . . .

then she puts it at the bottom of the stairs.

She tries the hallway and
then the bedroom. And then . . .

. . . aah! The bathroom is perfect!

That night, when Nancy is getting ready
for bed, she brushes her teeth and smiles
through the toothpaste at her painting.

The next morning, when Nancy goes
into the bathroom, she sees footprints!
　There are footprints on the bath mat!
　Footprints of all different shapes and sizes!
　Nancy looks around. There is nothing under
the bathtub and nothing behind the curtain.

Nancy decides to investigate.

ZOO

She waits at the bus stop,

talking to her neighbors, but she doesn't mention the footprints.

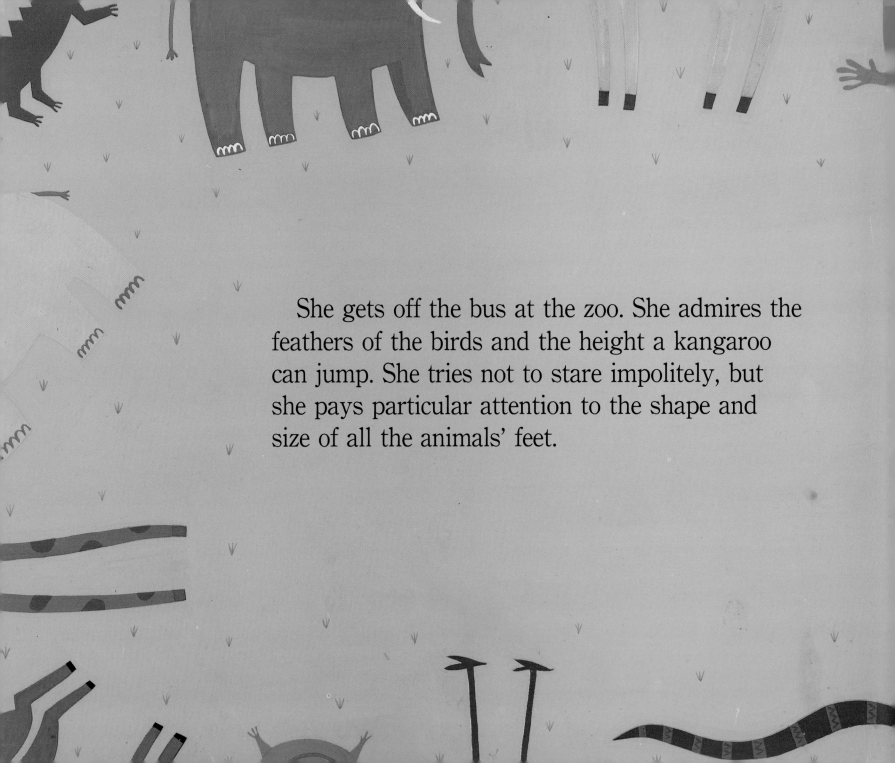

She gets off the bus at the zoo. She admires the feathers of the birds and the height a kangaroo can jump. She tries not to stare impolitely, but she pays particular attention to the shape and size of all the animals' feet.

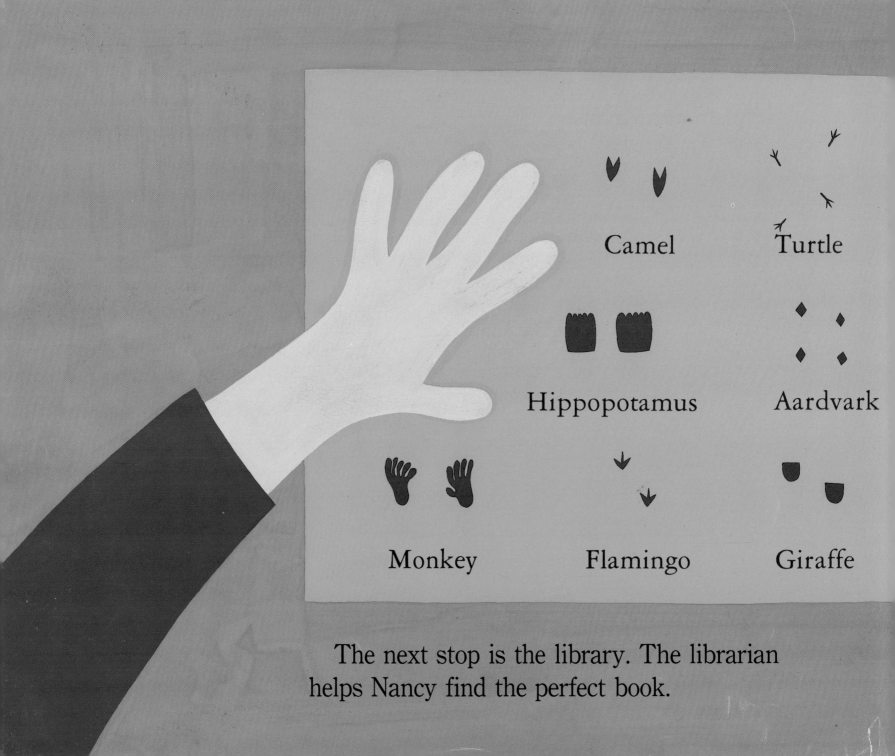

Camel

Turtle

Hippopotamus

Aardvark

Monkey

Flamingo

Giraffe

The next stop is the library. The librarian
helps Nancy find the perfect book.

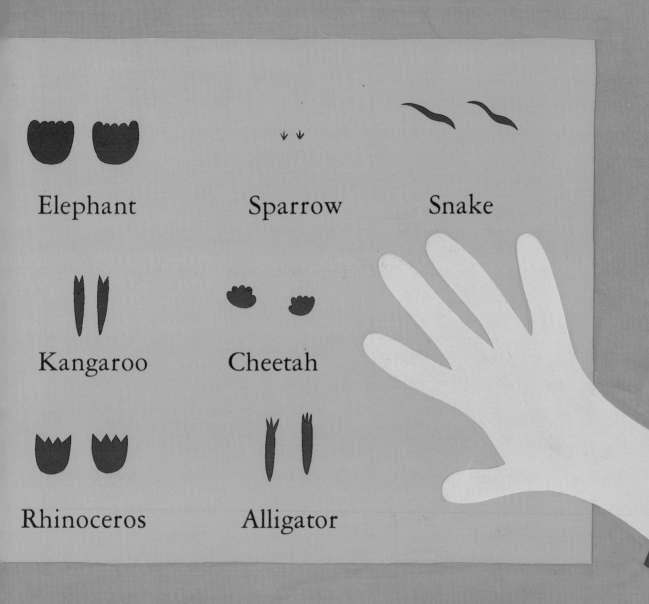

Elephant Sparrow Snake

Kangaroo Cheetah

Rhinoceros Alligator

Nancy recognizes many of the footprints she
saw in her bathroom. She decides to go home.

She walks up the path. What is that noise?

She opens the front door.
Is that a scurrying sound?

She goes into the kitchen and then into the hallway.

It is just as she suspected. Nancy climbs the stairs to the bathroom and opens the door.

The animals stop where they are, hardly daring to breathe,

Book One

Design and Technology
in metal and plastics

Book One

Design and Technology
in metal and plastics

J D Wolchover Design and Technology Teacher Wimbledon College

Nelson

Thomas Nelson and Sons Ltd
Lincoln Way Windmill Road
Sunbury-on-Thames Middlesex TW16 7HP
P.O. Box 73146 Nairobi Kenya
P.O. Box 943 95 Church Street Kingston Jamaica

Thomas Nelson (Australia) Ltd
19-39 Jeffcott Street West Melbourne Victoria 3003

Thomas Nelson and Sons (Canada) Ltd
81 Curlew Drive Don Mills Ontario

Thomas Nelson (Nigeria) Ltd
8 Ilupeju Bypass PMB 1303 Ikeja Lagos

© Julian Wolchover 1977
First published in 1977
ISBN 0 17 431095 1

Design by Janet Sterling

Illustration by R & B Art

Printed in Hong Kong.

Acknowledgements

Thanks are due to the following for help with the
preparation of illustrations: Elliot Machine
Equipment Ltd, Gale Brothers (Engineers) Ltd,
James Neill (Sheffield) Ltd, Prima Glassfibre
Materials Ltd, Record Ridgway Education Service,
Rhodes Flamefast Ltd, H. S. Walsh and Sons Ltd.

For photographs, acknowledgements are due to:
Barnaby's Picture Library (pp. 7, 8 upper left, 9
lower left and centre, 26, 46 left, 94, 96 centre
right), Bath City Council (p. 9 lower right), The
British Aircraft Corporation (p. 96 bottom), The
British Railways Board (p. 96 centre left), Chile
Copper Ltd (p. 23), Courtaulds Ltd (p. 90). The
Design Council (p. 8 lower left), The Electricity
Council (p. 96 top), Gale Brothers (Engineers) Ltd
(p. 82), John Goldblatt, for *Craft* magazine (p. 76),
Robert Golden (p. 66), Habitat Designs Ltd (p. 93
right), Heal and Son Ltd (p. 9 top), Peter Hurst-
Smith (p. 93), Index Photographic Library (pp. 23
upper right and bottom, 39, 56), *Integrated Craft*
(p. 64 left), Mike Kenna (pp. 19, 64 right, 86), The
National Spice Information Bureau (p. 92), Prima
Glassfibre Materials Ltd (p. 44), The Victoria and
Albert Museum (pp. 8 right, 46 right), Tim Wheeler
(p. 38), C. M. Wolchover (pp. 22, 23 upper left,
24, 28, 40, 47, 48, 52, 58, 60, 63, 68, 79, 80, 84).

Contents

Preface

This book is intended as an introduction to metal and plastics design and technology for the younger Secondary School or older Middle School child. Although the book as a whole constitutes a complete course of craftwork and theory, which is as important for the 11–13 year olds as it is for the G.C.E. and C.S.E. candidate, many teachers may find that their timetable does not allow the forty hours a year that are needed. It is quite reasonable in this situation to pick out key areas of work which will lay the foundations either for later fourth and fifth year courses or for leisure activities which will be followed for many years.

The jobs that I would recommend are:
1   Setting Hammer
2   Brass Key Tag
3   Small Dish
4   'Stained Glass' Decoration
5   Either Enamelled Pendant or Etched Pendant
6   Small Board Game
7   Egg Holder
8   Cast Aluminium Block
9   Bookends
10   One Group Project

In this way the children will work with most materials and basic processes covered by the course. They will also have to solve the design problems which are the basis of all meaningful practical work, and they will have to co-operate in a group project which will allow them to share ideas and arrive at solutions by discussion as well as by inspiration.

J. D. W.

Design

This book is not only about making things but also about solving the problems that come before anything can be made at all. This problem-solving activity is called 'designing'. To design something you have to have an idea of what you want it to do. You then have to decide what the article will be made of, how it will work and what it must look like in order to work well. This all sounds very involved, but it is not really very complicated. As an example, think about a seat.

What do you want? Something to sit on. You can sit on an old crate, but that is hardly a good answer to the problem.

seat

not very comfortable

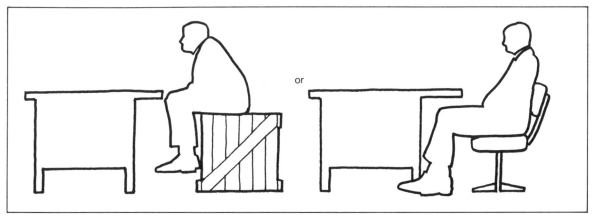

or

Design

The questions you must ask yourself are:
What is it for?
How will it be used?
How will it do this best?
How will it be put together?
What will it be made from and why?
This is the stage of *functional* design. Next comes the part that you probably think of when you hear the word 'design' mentioned, the stage of *aesthetic* design.

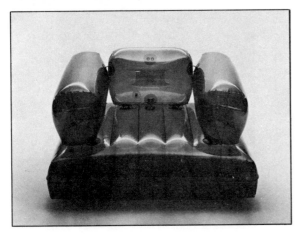

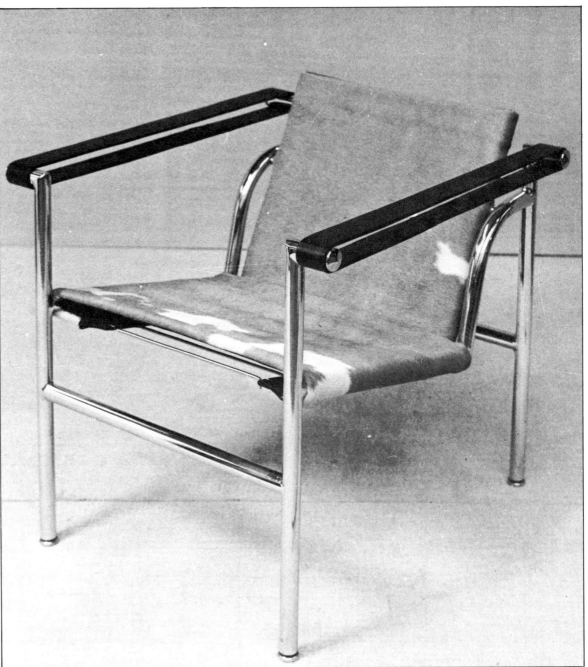

Now the questions you must ask yourself
are:
Where will it be used?
Who will use it?
What will it look like?
What will it 'feel' like?
**Will it look as if it is made from the
right materials?**
**Will it look right in the place where
it is to be used?**

When you have the answers to all these
questions, and more that you will think of,
only then can you start to make the object
successfully.

9

Metals I

Iron and steel

One of the most widely used and cheapest of all metals is mild steel. All of us use things made of mild steel every day of our lives, from the buses we ride in to the tins some of our food comes out of.

Steel is a mixture of iron with a very small amount of carbon. It starts off as **iron ore,** which is dug out of the ground. This ore is taken to the steel works where it is put into a **blast furnace** with coke and limestone. It is heated up, and air is blasted through it to melt the iron out of the ore. The limestone mixes with the unwanted bits of rock in the ore to form slag. Carbon from the coke mixes with the molten iron, which is poured into a **basic oxygen converter** and has pure oxygen blown across its surface. This mixes with some of the carbon to make carbon monoxide and carbon dioxide gases, leaving the right amount of carbon mixed with the molten iron in the converter to make steel. The steel can now be poured into moulds to make blocks called **ingots.** These are then rolled out into the different shaped bars, rods and sheets of steel needed by the manufacturing industries and craftsmen who use steel.

Many different sorts of steel are made, depending on the use to which the steel is to be put. They all contain different amounts of carbon, and also other materials in small quantities which are added to the converter along with the molten iron from the blast furnace. Most

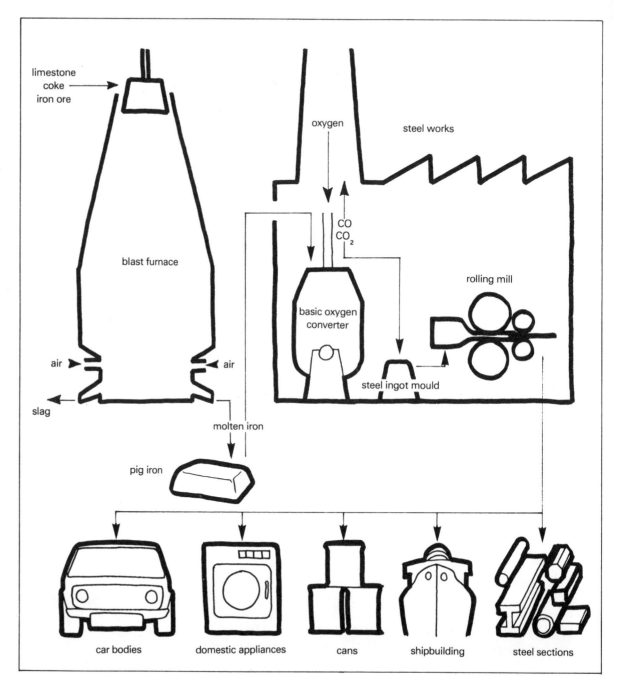

limestone
coke
iron ore

oxygen

steel works

blast furnace

CO
CO_2

rolling mill

basic oxygen converter

air

air

steel ingot mould

slag

molten iron

pig iron

car bodies

domestic appliances

cans

shipbuilding

steel sections

of the steel is called **mild steel,** which is the type of steel used in most motor car bodies, washing machine cases and so on.

Aluminium

Aluminium is an element. It is a silvery-coloured metal which is very light in weight. It is soft and it cuts very easily, but it does tend to clog the teeth of saws and files. It conducts heat and electricity very well, but it melts at a relatively low temperature, about 730°C. It is malleable and ductile (it can be shaped by hammering or drawing out), but in its pure state it is not very strong. It is mostly used mixed with other metals, and in this form it is strong but still very light. As alloys (mixtures) it is used for such different purposes as frying pans and the covering for Concorde!

As a craft metal it can be turned very easily on a lathe, as long as the cutting tool is kept well cooled with paraffin or soluble oil. In sheet form it can be used for any of the silversmith's processes except soldering. It is very difficult to join aluminium except by using rivets or nuts and bolts.

Aluminium is made from an ore called **bauxite,** but the process to extract the metal from the ore is very complex and uses a very large amount of electricity. For this reason you will usually find aluminium smelting plants near hydro-electric power stations because these can provide enough power at a relatively low cost.

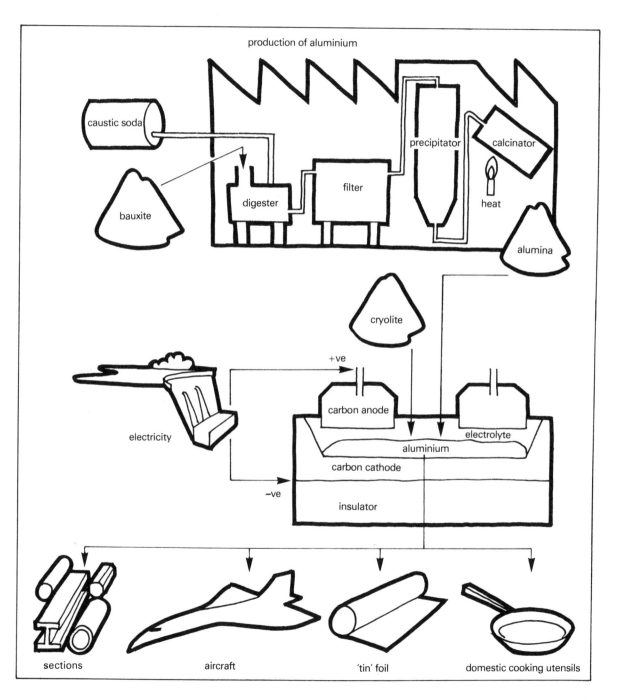

production of aluminium

caustic soda

precipitator

calcinator

bauxite

digester

filter

heat

alumina

cryolite

+ve

carbon anode

electrolyte

electricity

aluminium

carbon cathode

−ve

insulator

sections   aircraft   'tin' foil   domestic cooking utensils

Marking Tools

Before you can make anything you must 'mark out' the job on to the material you are using. This means that you draw on to the material the shape of the piece you wish to cut, file or drill.

The tools used for marking out are usually the following.

Scriber

This is made from silver steel or tool steel, and is a sharp pointed piece of rod held in a handle which allows you to grip it firmly. The point has to be very hard so that it will scratch the surface of the material being marked. The scratched line is the one you will be working to, and it is very fine.

Try square

This is made of cast steel and is used for measuring and marking right angles. It consists of a stock and a blade which are fitted together at right angles (90 degrees).

Steel rule

This is a ruler made from either cast steel or stainless steel, and it is very accurate. It is marked in millimetres and centimetres. The markings start at the end so that you can measure right into corners.

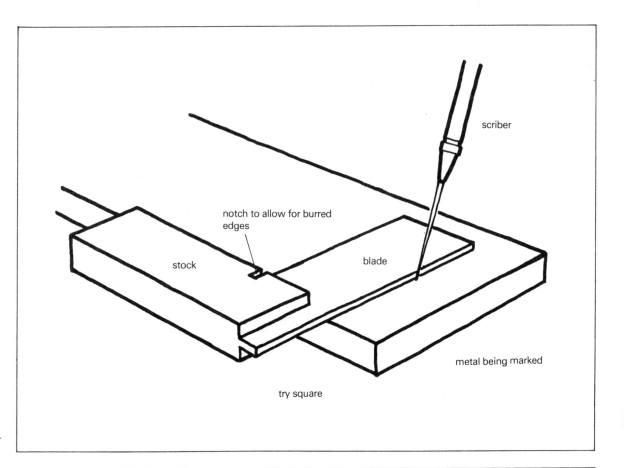

scriber

notch to allow for burred edges

stock

blade

metal being marked

try square

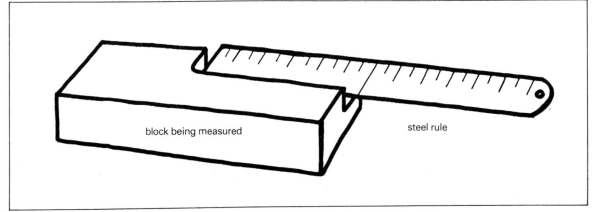

block being measured

steel rule

The marking tools described so far are the most basic ones, used for nearly every job you will do. There are others, among them those for marking circles and for marking the centres of holes to be drilled.

Dividers

These are used just like the compasses you use for geometry. The difference is that these have two points and they are very sharp so that they make a very fine, clear line.

Centre punch

This is like a very thick scriber in shape. The point is placed on the mark of the centre of the hole or circle and you hit the other end with a hammer. If you are marking a circle you must not hit the punch very hard. If you are marking the centre of a hole, hit the punch firmly just once. This makes a depression in the surface of the metal into which the point of a drill will fit.

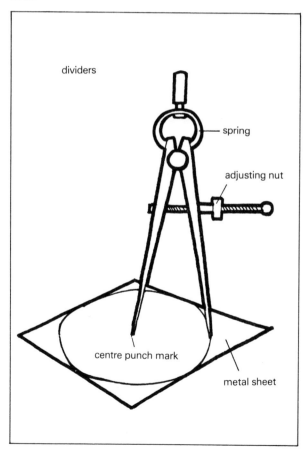

dividers

spring

adjusting nut

centre punch mark

metal sheet

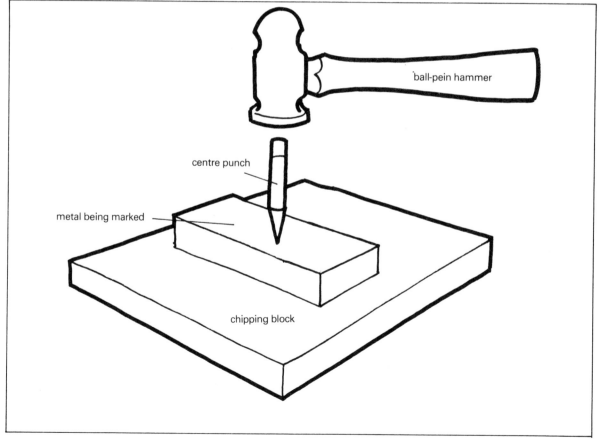

ball-pein hammer

centre punch

metal being marked

chipping block

Cutting Metals

In order to make things we must cut and shape the materials we are using. The tools we use for cutting metals and other materials are saws of various types, and snips or shears. The basic saw we use is called the **hacksaw.** There are two sorts of hacksaw, the adjustable hacksaw which will take different sized blades, and the **junior hacksaw** which takes a single, small size of blade.

Whatever materials you are going to cut, it is very important to select the right type of blade. For cutting thin, hard metals use a blade with a 'fine pitch', which means it has many small teeth to every centimetre of its length. For cutting large sections or soft materials you should choose a coarse-pitch blade with fewer teeth per centimetre.

A useful rule for choosing saw blades is to select one which will have at least three teeth always in contact with the surface you are cutting. You must always put the blade into the saw frame with the teeth pointing away from the handle so that you cut with the tool when you push it away from you.

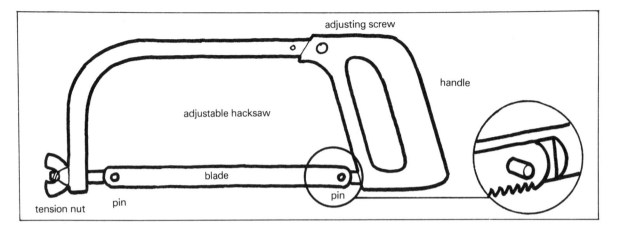

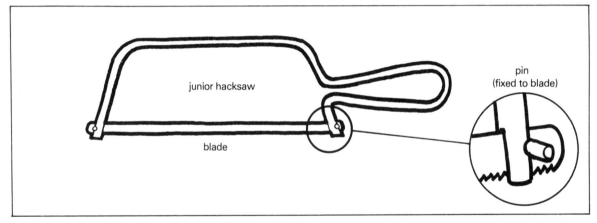

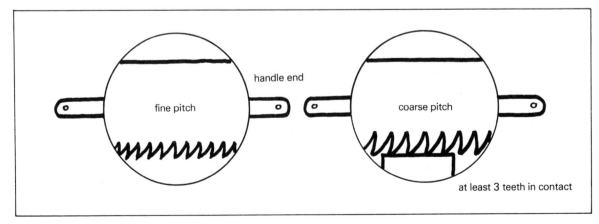

Coping saw

This saw is used mostly in woodwork for cutting intricate shapes. It may also be used to cut plastic sheet materials as long as they are not too thin. The saw has a coarse-pitch, replaceable blade which can be turned to any angle so that difficult shapes can be cut out. The blades are very thin, so great care must be taken when you use this type of saw. If you are very careful you can also use a coping saw to cut shapes in soft metals such as brass or copper.

Snips

These are like very strong scissors and are used for cutting thin sheet metals. Even the finest hacksaw blades are too coarse for thin metal such as we use for making bowls and dishes. So we use snips, which come in many shapes and sizes. They are used just as scissors are for cutting paper, and may be used right up to a scribed line. You should not try to use them for cutting thick metals because this will only make them blunt. The thickest metal you should cut with snips is 1 mm to 1.5 mm thick.

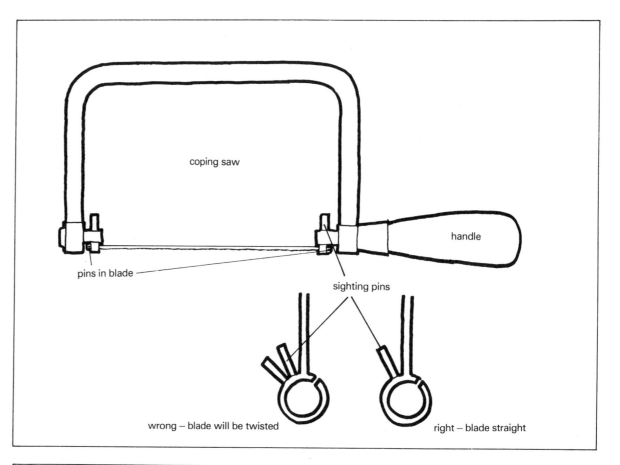

coping saw

handle

pins in blade

sighting pins

wrong – blade will be twisted

right – blade straight

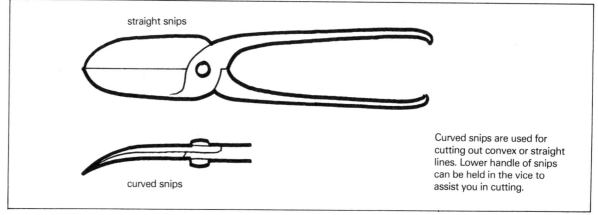

straight snips

curved snips

Curved snips are used for cutting out convex or straight lines. Lower handle of snips can be held in the vice to assist you in cutting.

Shaping Tools

Files

When a piece of metal or other material has been cut to its approximate shape it then has to be finished off to the lines scribed on it. To do this we use tools called **files.**

Files are made of cast steel and are very hard because they have to be harder than the materials they have to shape. As well as being very hard they are also very brittle. This means that they break very easily, so care has to be taken not to bang them too hard. A file is held by a wooden handle fitted to the end called the **tang** of the file. This part is not hard or brittle. The file must always have a handle on it because the tang is sharp.

By holding the file in one hand and lightly guiding it with the other, strokes can be made across the work you are shaping. This is called **cross-filing.**

Another way of filing is called **draw-filing.** To do this you hold the file across the work and draw it back and forth along the edge you are finishing off. This gives the surface of the materials a very fine 'finish'.

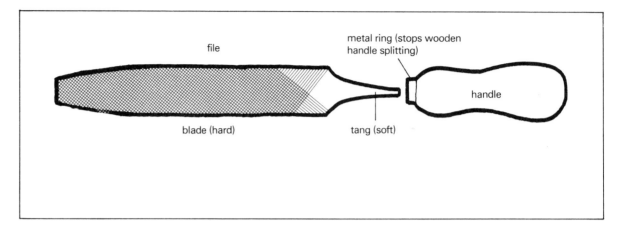

file

metal ring (stops wooden handle splitting)

handle

blade (hard)

tang (soft)

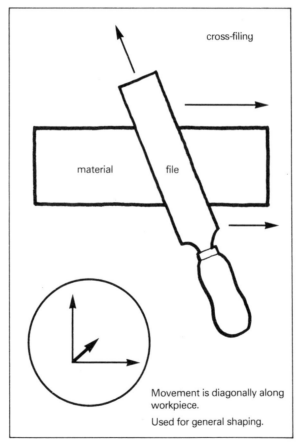

cross-filing

material

file

Movement is diagonally along workpiece.

Used for general shaping.

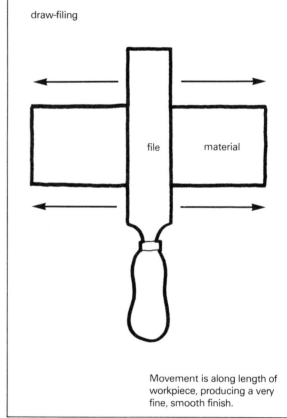

draw-filing

file

material

Movement is along length of workpiece, producing a very fine, smooth finish.

Files come in many shapes and sizes and qualities of 'cut'. The cut of a file is the number of teeth per centimetre cut into its surface. These teeth work in the same way as the teeth of a saw, cutting away small amounts of material with every forward stroke. Sometimes small pieces of material become stuck in the teeth; this is called **pinning** and can be removed by using a stiff wire brush called a **file card**.

The most usual shapes of files are **flat, hand** (which is similar to flat but has parallel sides along its whole length), **half-round** (which would be D-shaped if you could cut it across), **round, square,** and **triangular.** They come in several lengths, the most usual in school being 10", 8" and 6". The cuts range from rough to smooth and include one called **second cut** and another called **bastard cut.** You choose a file according to whether the job is large or small and whether you have to do rough shaping or fine finishing. To file the edge of a brass name plate to a fine finish you would most likely choose a 6" smooth hand file. To roughly shape the inside of a circular hole in a thick piece of steel you would choose a 10" second cut half-round file.

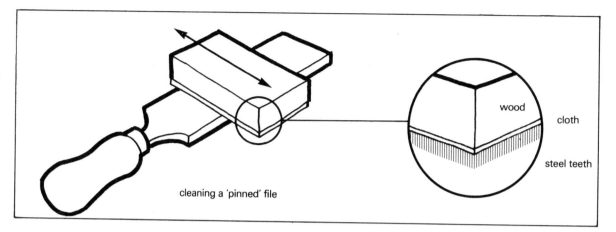

wood
cloth
steel teeth

cleaning a 'pinned' file

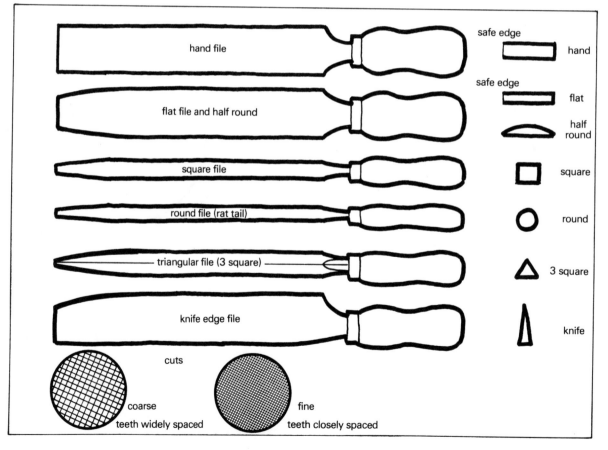

hand file

flat file and half round

square file

round file (rat tail)

triangular file (3 square)

knife edge file

safe edge
hand

safe edge
flat

half round

square

round

3 square

knife

cuts

coarse
teeth widely spaced

fine
teeth closely spaced

Shaping Tools

Drills

In order to cut holes in metals or other materials we must use **drills.** These are tools made of **cast steel** (for cutting soft materials) or **high speed steel** (for cutting hard materials such as metals). They are straight-sided rods, with grooves spiralling up their sides. They have sharp points at one end. The pointed end does the cutting and the other end, called the **shank,** which has no grooves, is held in the drilling machine. The drill turns, and as it does you lower it into the material in which you want to cut the hole. The pointed end has two cutting edges on it which slice into the material being drilled.

You must take care when using a drilling machine not to allow the drill point to become too hot because this will blunt it. For many metals you must use a special **cutting oil** to cool the drill as you make the hole.

Safety
One very important fact that you must beware of when you use a drilling machine is that it can be dangerous. In order to avoid accidents to your eyes from flying pieces of the material you are drilling, always wear safety goggles. Drilling machines are revolving at high speed near your face, so if you have long hair always tie it back or it could get caught and pulled out.

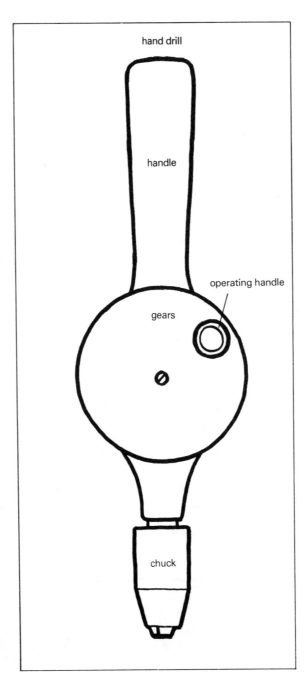

hand drill

handle

operating handle

gears

chuck

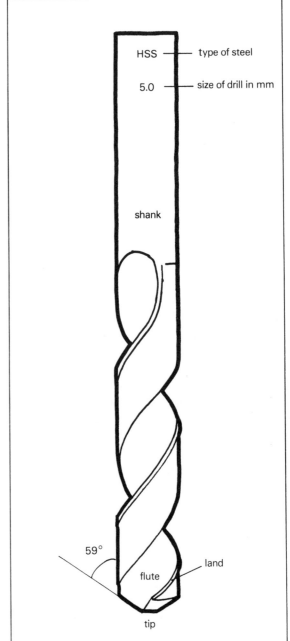

HSS ——— type of steel

5.0 ——— size of drill in mm

shank

59°

flute

land

tip

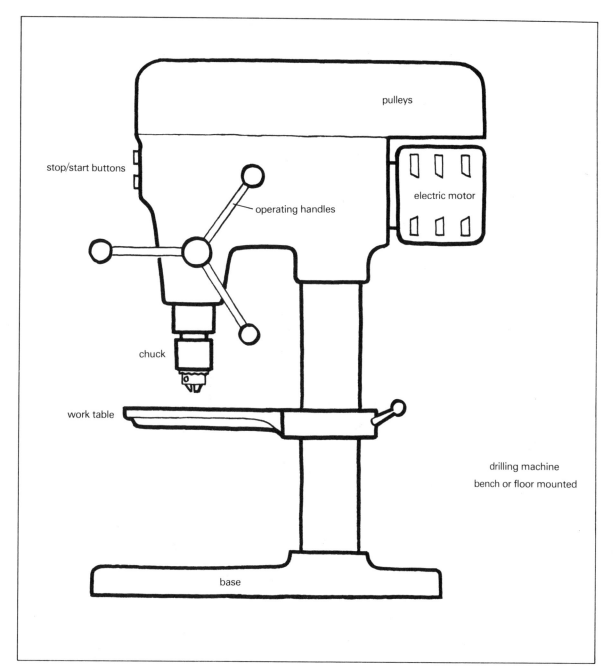

pulleys

stop/start buttons

operating handles

electric motor

chuck

work table

drilling machine
bench or floor mounted

base

Setting Hammer

This is a small hammer which is used when you make jewellery, for fixing stones on to rings or brooches and also for decorating the surface of metals by making small marks on it. The design of the hammer head is governed by its size and the need for it to have one end flat and the other wedge-shaped. The part of the hammer which allows you to provide your own solution is the handle and the way it is fixed to the hammer head. You must ask yourself certain questions in order to decide on the best handle to use and the right way of fitting it to the head. These questions are:

How long must the handle be?
How wide must it be?
What is the best material to make it out of?
How can it be fixed firmly into place?

You can answer these questions by looking at several other hammers in the workshop at school and seeing how they are held and used. Your hammer will be a small version of one (or more) of these.

To make the Hammer Head

You will need: a Scriber, try square, steel rule, hacksaw, 8" hand file (2nd cut), Mild Steel 10 mm square, 45 mm long.

1 File one end flat and square.
2 Mark out the job from the drawing.
(All the measurements are given to you on the drawing.)

hammer head

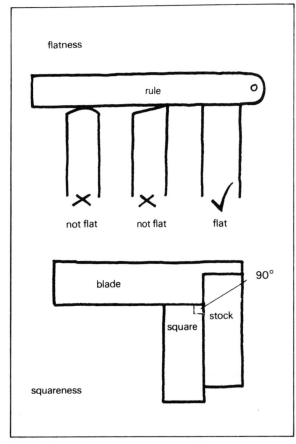

flatness

rule

not flat   not flat   flat

blade   90°

square   stock

squareness

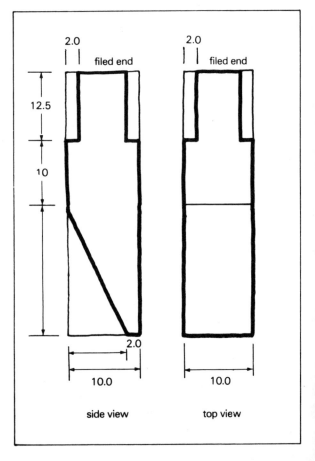

2.0   filed end   2.0   filed end

12.5

10

2.0

10.0   10.0

side view   top view

3   Saw the metal to length and then saw the wedge-shaped end.
4   File the wedge-shaped end to the lines you have marked.

5   File the edges off the other end.
6   Draw file the hammer head on all sides. Use a smooth file for this.
7   Wipe oil all over the head to stop rust.

Now you have to make the handle that you think is the most suitable one for your hammer. One possible solution is to use a plain rod of mild steel 5 mm in diameter and 150 mm long. This can be fixed to the head by drilling a hole in the hammer head and fixing the rod into it either by using solder or by making a screw thread on the handle and another in the hole. The two pieces then fit together like a nut and bolt.

Wood or plastic might provide you with a different solution.

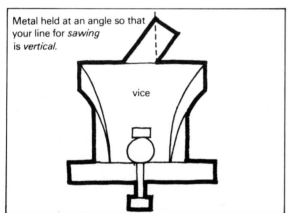

Metal held at an angle so that your line for *sawing* is *vertical*.

vice

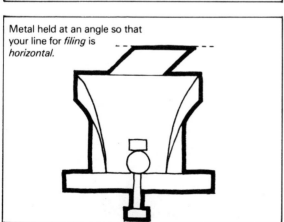

Metal held at an angle so that your line for *filing* is *horizontal*.

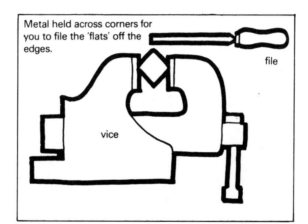

Metal held across corners for you to file the 'flats' off the edges.

file

vice

Oil stops rusting.

oil can

rag

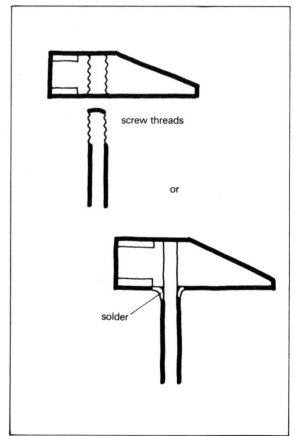

screw threads

or

solder

Metals 2

Copper

Copper is an element. It is a reddish-coloured metal, very soft, malleable and ductile (it can be shaped by hammering and can be drawn into wire), and it is an excellent conductor of heat and electricity. As a sheet metal we can use copper to make almost any hollow form by hammering it on to a variety of shaped tools called **stakes** (see pages 28 and 31) or on to a wooden block. When hammered in this way the copper becomes **work hardened,** so we have to soften it again by a process called **annealing** (see pages 34 and 37).

Brass

Brass is a golden-coloured alloy (mixture) of two metals both of which are elements, copper and zinc. The proportions in which they are mixed are usually about 60% copper to 40% zinc. It is a relatively soft metal, easy to work with but also easily damaged. It feels quite slippery when you file it, and this property is used to make bearings in machinery, because any metal that is slippery is useful if you are designing a machine which has two parts moving against one another. Another property of brass is that it is easy to polish it to a mirror-like finish, and so it is ideal for making small pieces of attractive jewellery. Unfortunately it is much more expensive than steel, so you must take great care not to spoil it by doing up your vice too tightly or by dropping it on to the floor or bench top. If you do take care you will achieve a very professional appearance to your work.

22

Layout Blue

One of the problems you will come across when you work with metals is that of scribing an accurate line that you can see easily on the surface of the metal. This is because when you scratch the surface there is no change in colour but only the brightness of the fresh mark which can become dull very quickly. To make the job of marking out easier, metalworkers use a dye to colour the surface of the metal blue. This dye is a solution of copper sulphate in a spirit which evaporates very quickly. If you lightly paint the surface of a clean piece of metal·with **layout blue** the dye will dry in a few seconds. When you now use the scriber on it the lines you make will show up very clearly indeed against the blue colouring. When the job is finished you can clean off the blue with meths.

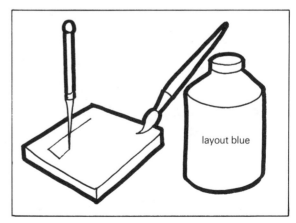

Polishing Metals and Plastics

Polishing is a 'finishing' operation which leaves the surface of the material you are using perfectly smooth and shiny.

Hand polishing

Hand polishing can be done by rubbing the surface to be polished with emery cloth. Emery cloth is a mild abrasive, that is, it cuts the surface of the material. If you use very fine emery cloth the scratches are very close together and very shallow, so you get a smooth surface. If the emery cloth is of a grade such that it feels like powder on the surface then the metal becomes shiny when rubbed over. You can finish off this polishing by using liquid metal polish for a really shiny surface. This process takes a long time and a great deal of effort.

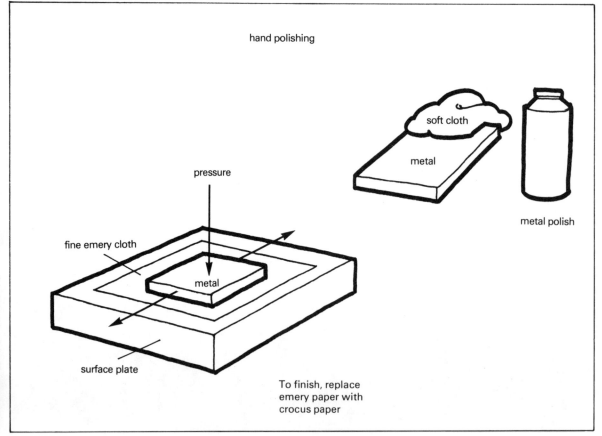

hand polishing

soft cloth

metal

metal polish

pressure

fine emery cloth

metal

surface plate

To finish, replace emery paper with crocus paper

Machine polishing

Machine polishing is used because hand polishing takes so long. The machines do the rubbing for us. They are called **buffing machines.** Simply, they are electric motors with a mop made of discs of calico on the spindle. The motor spins the mop which you coat with an abrasive wax. If you hold your metal or plastic against the revolving mop the surface becomes polished. To obtain the best results we can use mops of different materials which are softer and wax polishes which contain finer abrasive materials. One of these is called 'Rouge' and is red in colour.

When you use a buffing machine your work will get very hot. Do not hold it in a piece of rag. Put it down to cool. Always wear goggles.

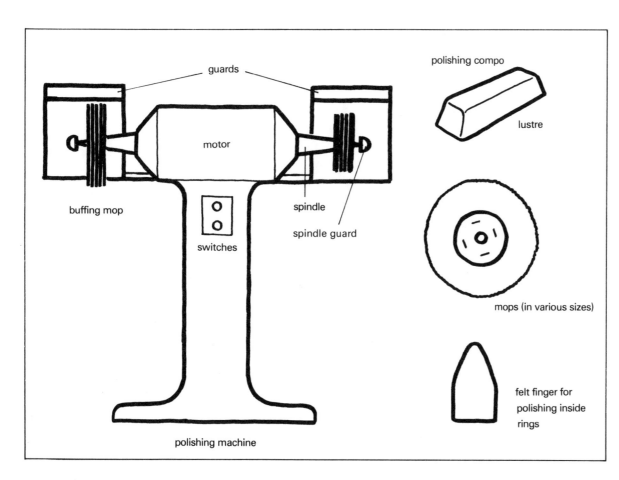

guards

polishing compo

lustre

motor

buffing mop

spindle

spindle guard

switches

mops (in various sizes)

felt finger for polishing inside rings

polishing machine

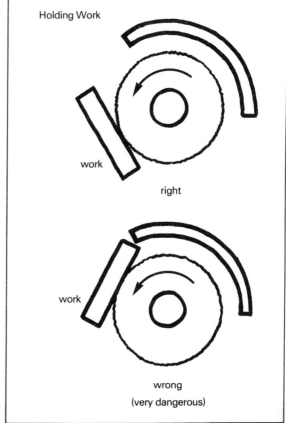

Holding Work

work

right

work

wrong
(very dangerous)

Brass Key Tag

We usually keep keys on rings. This is to keep them all together so that they are easier to keep track of. Often we decorate these key-rings with tags of one sort or another. Some tags are only for decoration, but others are to tell us what the keys will lock or unlock.

In order to make a purely decorative key tag we can use a metal which has a pleasing appearance not unlike gold. This metal is Brass, which has a rich yellow colour and which can be polished easily to a mirror-like finish. A key tag must be small so that it is not awkward to carry in your pocket, and there are other considerations such as not having sharp corners to tear your clothes. For your design try to think of simple shapes taken from nature or the townscape around you (leaves or chimney pots perhaps) and which are symmetrical about a vertical or a horizontal line.

To make the key tag

You will need: Layout blue, scriber, rule, files of various cross sections, centre punch, 3 mm drill, scissors. Brass sheet 1.2 mm thick by 30 mm by 25 mm. A piece of card the same size as the brass.

1   When you have decided on your design draw it on to the piece of card. Cut it out with the scissors, and then cut it in half along the line about which it is symmetrical.

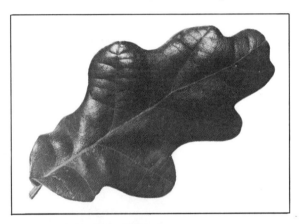

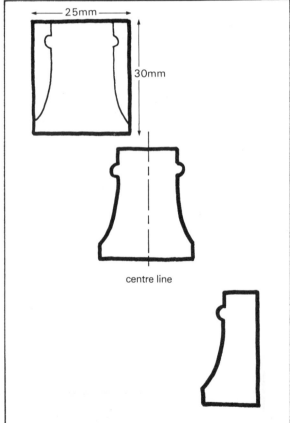

25mm

30mm

centre line

2   Paint a thin coat of layout blue on to the piece of brass.

3   Mark a centre line on the metal to match the one on the card. Put the half shape (card) down and mark round it. Turn it over to mark the other half.

4   File the metal exactly to the line you have now drawn. (Protect the metal from contact with the vice jaws with card.)

5   Clean off the blue. Polish the surfaces and edges of the metal.

6   Mark a spot on the centre line near the top edge and centre punch it. Drill a 3 mm diameter hole with a hand drill.

Safety

Wear goggles when polishing. If you have to use a power drill hold the metal in a hand vice and wear goggles.

layout blue

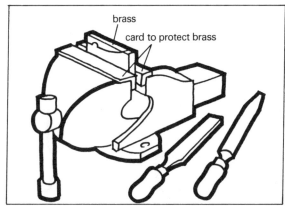

brass

card to protect brass

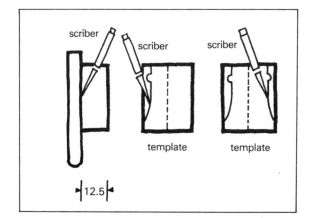

scriber

scriber

scriber

template

template

12.5

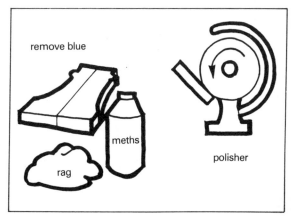

remove blue

meths

rag

polisher

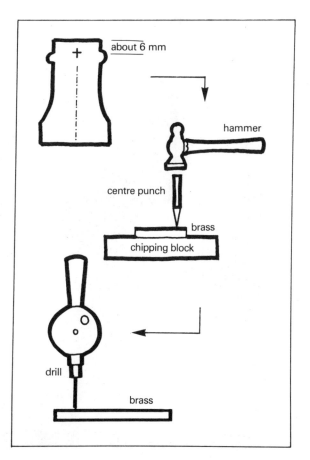

about 6 mm

hammer

centre punch

brass

chipping block

drill

brass

Sheet Metal

Gilding metal

When making decorative articles you might wish to bend or shape the metal in other ways than cutting or filing. Also you might want a metal that is gold in colour but not as yellow as brass. A metal which is suitable is called **gilding metal.** Like brass it is made from copper and zinc, but mixed in different proportions. It polishes well to a fine finish. When thick it can be used for rings and other jewellery, when thin it can be made into dishes. It is both ductile and malleable, and these properties make it an ideal metal for learning about silversmithing, which is the art of making objects out of sheet metal, usually out of silver.

Stakes

In order to shape sheet metal to make curved objects, the metal has to be hammered out. The tools on to which the metal is hammered are called **stakes,** and they are made from iron or steel. The surface of the stake is curved to the shape the craftsman wants to form the metal into, so he must have a selection of different stakes. The surfaces of the stakes must be kept polished and free from dents and scratches, so that the metal will not be spoilt when it is hammered. This is because the metal is squashed between the hammer and the stake, so that any marks on either tool will be transferred to the metal.

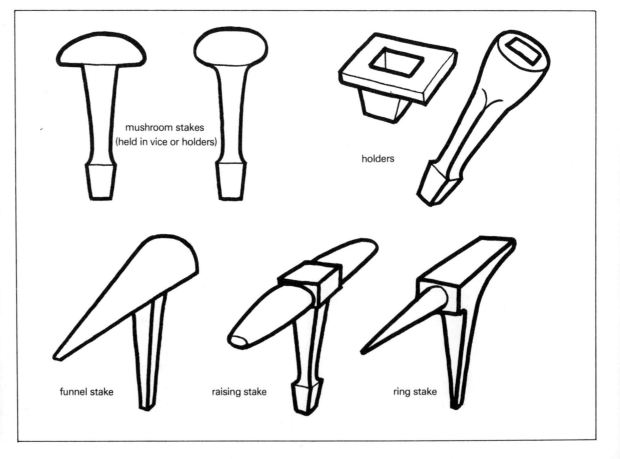

mushroom stakes
(held in vice or holders)

holders

funnel stake

raising stake

ring stake

Planishing hammer

One of the basic silversmith's tools is the **planishing hammer.** It is made from cast steel and has two highly polished faces. One, the most used, is round and flat. The other is square and convex, for hammering concave curves. The handle is usually made of hickory wood.

The process of planishing stretches the metal slightly over a stake. As you work the metal with the hammer you must move it round so that every part is evenly touched by the hammer. You must always make sure that the hammer is striking on to the same part of the stake, otherwise the curve may be different and the object will become uneven. The hammering leaves small flat marks on the surface of the metal. These should be overlapped by the next mark and so on all round the object for the best results.

Hide mallet

Craftsmen use two sorts of tools to beat metal, hammers and mallets. Hammers are made of steel but mallets are made of wood, plastic, rubber or leather. The leather is called rawhide and is just like the 'Doggy Chews' sold in pet shops. It is used because it is softer than the metals you will hit with it and so it leaves no mark on the metal even though it will bend it.

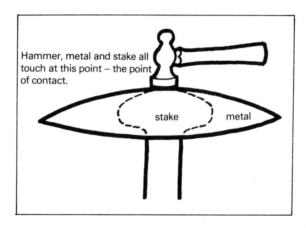

Hammer, metal and stake all touch at this point — the point of contact.

stake   metal

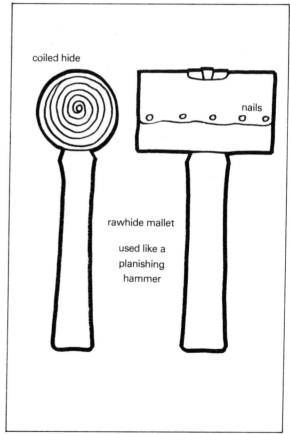

coiled hide

nails

rawhide mallet

used like a planishing hammer

round/flat faced   square/convex faced

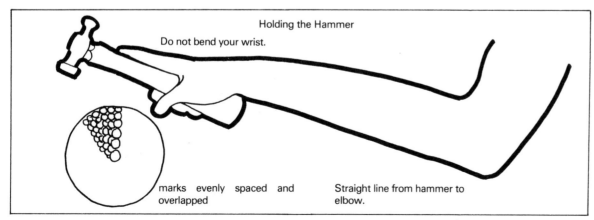

Holding the Hammer
Do not bend your wrist.

marks evenly spaced and overlapped

Straight line from hammer to elbow.

Napkin Ring

In any simple ring shape which is left open at the ends, there is plenty of opportunity for you to explore the possibilities of shaping the ends so that they appear to interlock with one another even though they do not actually touch. If you keep to simple shapes you can try them out by drawing them on paper and then cutting them out with scissors and bending the paper round into a ring. When you have found a shape that you find pleasing, and one which has no sharp points to catch the cloth of the napkin which will go through the ring, you can transfer your design to a piece of gilding metal.

To make your napkin ring

You will need: Layout blue, scriber, saw and/or files of different shapes and sizes, a hide mallet, large ring stake, gilding metal 1.6 mm thick by 25 mm by 125 mm.

1   Blue the ends of the strip and mark out.
2   Cut out and file the shaped ends to the line you have marked.

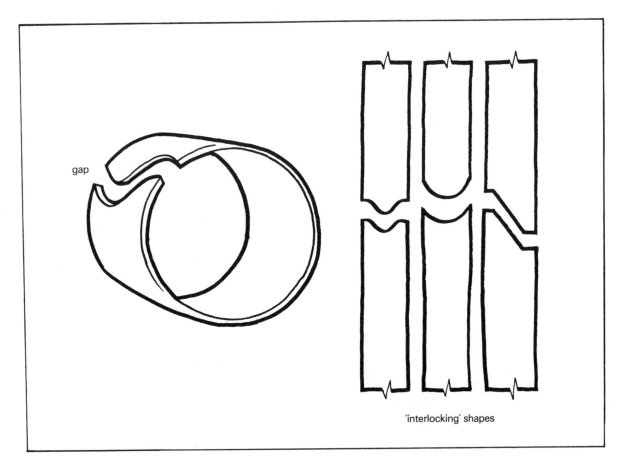

gap

'interlocking' shapes

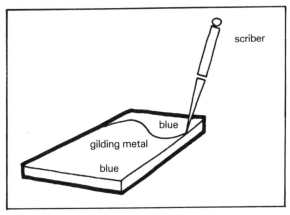

scriber
blue
gilding metal
blue

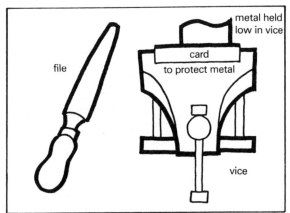

metal held low in vice
card
to protect metal
file
vice

30

3 Drawfile all the edges so that they are 'square' to the faces of the metal strip.

4 Polish the other side on the buffing machine. This will be the outside of the ring.

5 Bend the strip into a ring round the ring stake. Use a hide mallet for this.

6 Polish the outside again and the inside with metal polish.

Safety
Wear your goggles!

Now you may, if you wish, put a texture on to the surface of the ring by using a planishing hammer lightly on it on the ring stake, or by using the wedge-shaped end of your setting hammer to make small straight marks in the surface. If you make sure that the face of the hammer you choose is perfectly polished, you will only have to go over the surface with liquid metal polish afterwards to bring out a really deep shine.

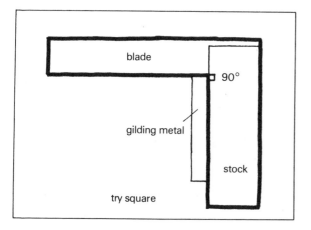

blade

90°

gilding metal

stock

try square

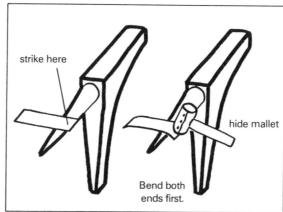

strike here

hide mallet

Bend both ends first.

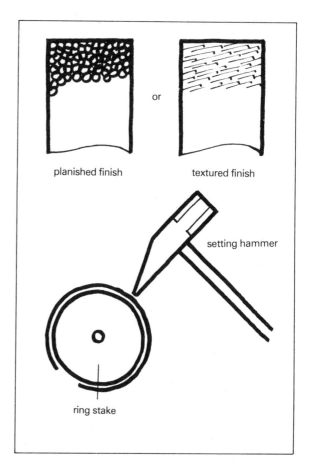

planished finish

or

textured finish

setting hammer

ring stake

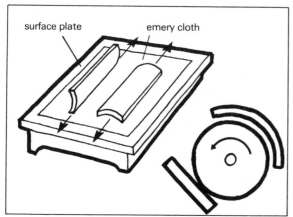

surface plate

emery cloth

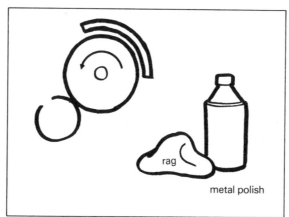

rag

metal polish

Joining Metals

There are many ways in which we can join two or more pieces of metal together. The way most often used by silversmiths or coppersmiths is called **soldering.** This can be done at either a high or a low temperature. Which you choose depends on what metals you are joining and how strong the joint needs to be. The solder you use for high-temperature, strong joints is **silver solder.** This is made from silver and copper, with some other materials added in very small amounts to help the solder to flow easily when it is molten. It is used to make good-looking joints in jewellery and silversmithing jobs as well as joining steel for some engineering jobs.

Soldering means the joining of two pieces by using molten metal as a 'glue'. This metal has to be able to melt at a lower temperature than the metals being joined. It also has to be able to flow into the joint and seal it completely. Silver solder can only do this if the edges to be joined touch each other with no visible gaps. The surface of the metal has to be kept clean because the solder can only stick to the cleanest surfaces. When metals are heated up they 'oxidize' on the surface. This layer of metal oxide prevents solder from sticking to it so we use a substance called **flux** to keep the surfaces to be joined free from oxidation. The flux we use with silver solder is made from powdered borax. Mixed with water, we can make it into a paste which we spread on the joint. We then heat the place to be joined with a blow torch until it is red hot. At this temperature the silver solder will melt and run into the joint.

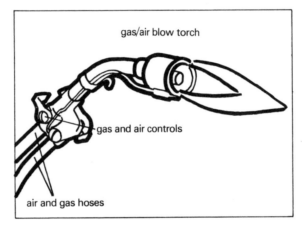

gas/air blow torch

gas and air controls

air and gas hoses

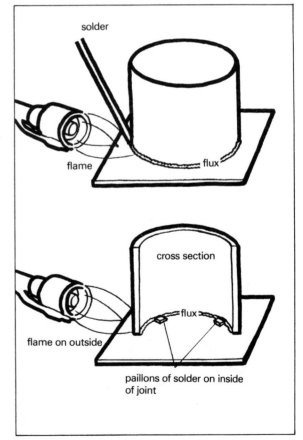

solder

flame

flux

cross section

flame on outside

flux

paillons of solder on inside of joint

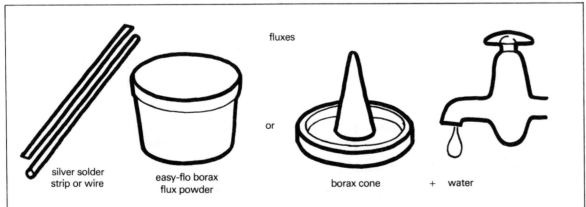

fluxes

or

silver solder strip or wire

easy-flo borax flux powder

borax cone

+ water

The other sort of soldering is called **soft soldering** because the solder is made of lead. This melts at only about 300°C, but it is not very strong. It is used a great deal to join tinplate and to fix electronic components together because higher temperatures would damage them. It can be put on in two ways. The first is by using a tool called a **soldering iron.** This is a sharpened piece of copper held on a long handle. The copper 'bit' is heated in a stove and this, when we put it on to the metal to be joined, provides enough heat for the solder to run. The other method is called **sweating.** To do this we first coat the surfaces to be joined with solder. Then we put them together and reheat them till the solder melts. This coating is called **tinning.** The flux we use when soft soldering is called Killed Spirits which is the old name for zinc chloride. Lead solder can be used to join most metals, but not aluminium.

Holding joints together

The biggest problem when soldering is to hold the edges of a joint together while you heat it up. To do this we use soft iron wire to make a parcel of the job. The important thing to remember when you wire up a job is to make a loop over the joint itself. If you don't you will solder the wire to the job! Pull the wire out to stretch it before you use it.

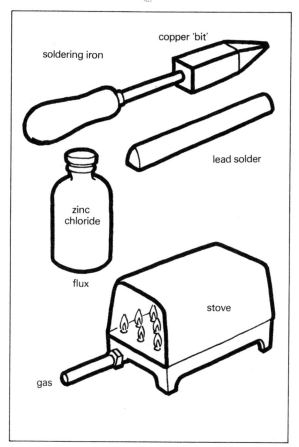

soldering iron
copper 'bit'
lead solder
zinc chloride
flux
stove
gas

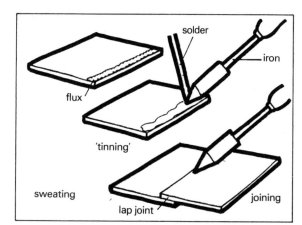

solder
iron
flux
'tinning'
sweating
lap joint
joining

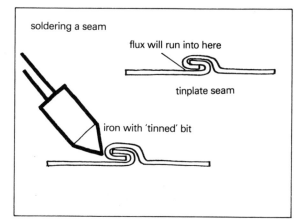

soldering a seam
flux will run into here
tinplate seam
iron with 'tinned' bit

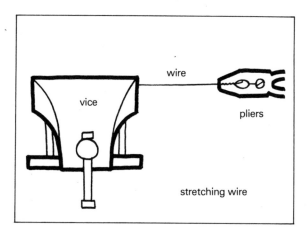

wire
vice
pliers
stretching wire

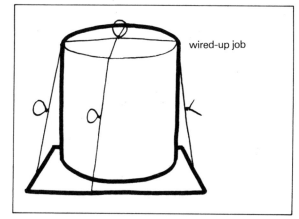

wired-up job

Annealing

If you hit a piece of metal with a hammer or squeeze it between rollers to shape it, or if you bend it, you will find that it gets hard. This is called **work-hardening,** and it happens to most metals. If you let the metal get too hard you will find that it becomes very difficult to work and that it may split or snap. You have probably broken a paper clip by repeatedly bending and straightening it. This happens because the wire gets harder and more brittle as you work it. You will also find that it gets hot when you do this. The heat is energy released by the molecules of the metal as they move against one another, and become packed closer together. To soften the metal you must move the molecules apart. We do this by heating the metal in a process called **annealing.**

Annealing is a very simple process to carry out. You must heat the metal up to red heat and then allow it to cool down. Some metals must be cooled slowly or they will remain hard from the shock to their structure from rapid cooling. Other metals such as silver or copper may be quenched in water (or dilute sulphuric acid) almost as soon as they have lost their redness. Brass is a metal which should be allowed to cool very slowly. As well as not cooling metals too quickly you should not heat them up too much either. Brass will crumble if you heat it too much and aluminium does not go red hot until it has melted! In order to tell the temperature for annealing aluminium you must rub soap all over it first.

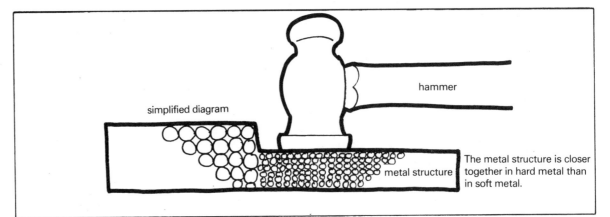

simplified diagram

hammer

metal structure

The metal structure is closer together in hard metal than in soft metal.

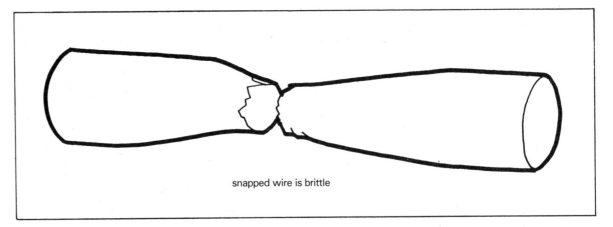

snapped wire is brittle

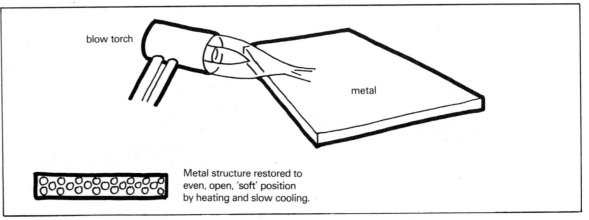

blow torch

metal

Metal structure restored to even, open, 'soft' position by heating and slow cooling.

When the soap goes brown the metal is at the right temperature and can be left to cool down slowly.

Pickling

When you pickle metals in acid after annealing them you must take special care. Putting hot metal into acid does not only clean off the oxides formed on the surface of the metal during heating; but the acid also splashes up as it boils as soon as the metal touches the surface.

Special precautions must be observed when pickling. Always wear your goggles to avoid acid splashing into your eyes. Wear rubber gloves whenever you handle acid or go near it with metals to be dipped in it. Never put red hot metal into acid.

Never put iron or steel into an acid bath; this contaminates it. Always handle hot or cold metal with brass tongs when dipping them in acids. If you do get acid splashes on your skin or clothes wash it off immediately with plenty of cold, clean water. Then tell your teacher.

If possible, pickle cold metal, after it has been quenched in water, by putting it in a small, deep container and heating this up over a bunsen burner, preferably in a closed fume cupboard. You will have better control over your work this way. After you have pickled metal in acid always wash the metal thoroughly in running cold water.

annealing aluminium

soap

aluminium

dark brown streaks from soap when heated to annealing temperature

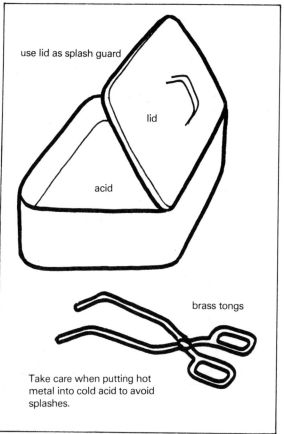

use lid as splash guard

lid

acid

brass tongs

Take care when putting hot metal into cold acid to avoid splashes.

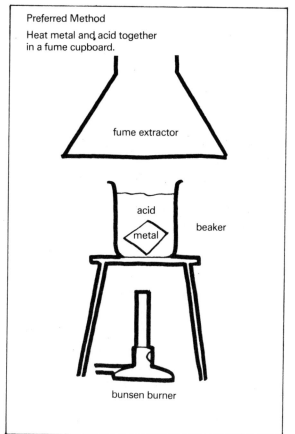

Preferred Method

Heat metal and acid together in a fume cupboard.

fume extractor

acid

metal

beaker

bunsen burner

Small Dish

We use small dishes at home for many things—as ash trays, sweet or nut dishes, or just for display. However we use them, they are all containers with the same basic shape. To make a shallow bowl form out of sheet metal we planish it on a mushroom stake. It is not necessary for the dish to be round to do this, and it can be raised from the surface on which it will stand by putting it on a small ring-shaped foot. The foot does not have to be round either, but it is easier to start from a round ring and alter the shape afterwards. The shape of the dish and the foot should complement each other.

To get some ideas for the design of your dish you could look at the shapes of broad leaves—leaves are still used in primitive societies as dishes. There are many shapes you can try out such as geometrical figures. The thing to take account of when choosing a shape for your dish is the purpose for which it will be used. It is no use having a small, thin dish to hold large, round pieces of fruit.

To make your dish

You will need: Marking tools, cutting tools (snips), smooth files, planishing hammer, mushroom stake, ring stake, binding wire, silver solder and borax flux, lead solder and killed spirits, copper sheet 1 mm thick by 75 mm square, brass strip 1.6 mm thick by 10 mm wide by length to suit your design.

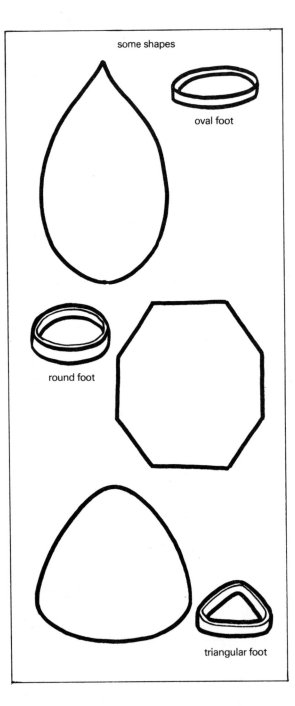

some shapes

oval foot

round foot

triangular foot

1   Mark out and cut out the shape of your dish on the copper. File and drawfile the edges to the lines you have marked.
2   Planish the copper to the shape you want.

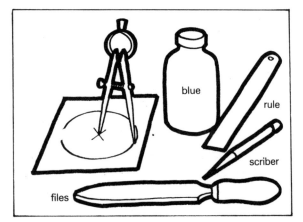

blue

rule

scriber

files

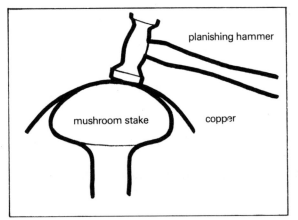

planishing hammer

mushroom stake

copper

3   Anneal and pickle the metal as it gets too hard to work easily.
4   Polish the dish inside and out.

5   Cut the brass strip to length. File the ends square. Form into a ring.
6   Wire up, flux and solder the joint in the ring. Clean up the joint with files and then do any shaping you want to.

7   'Fit' the foot to the dish so that it touches at all the necessary points.
8   Tin the edges of the foot and the points on the dish where they touch. Wire them together in place and warm them up until the solder runs.
9   Clean up the joint when it is cool and polish all over.

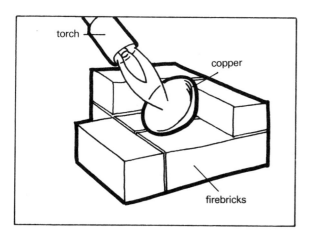

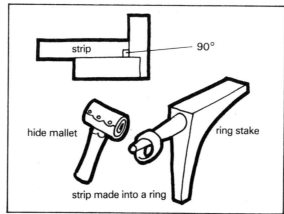

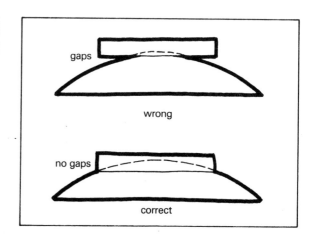

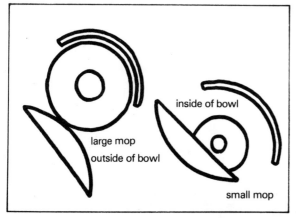

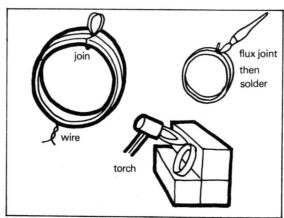

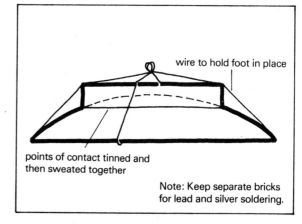

Plastics

The word 'Plastic' makes us think of cheap products such as bags or buckets. In fact there are as many different plastics materials as there are uses to which they can be put. The greatest revolution in materials has happened in the plastics industry. The reason for this is that plastics are 'synthetic' materials, that is, they are man-made. At first plastics were seen as a cheap alternative to metal and wood for a limited number of uses. Now there are some plastics which can be used very attractively as craft materials.

All plastics have the same basic chemical form. They consist of long molecules joined together in different ways. It is the long chain structure which makes them plastics or **polymers,** and it is the way these chains are connected that determines how the plastic can be used.

There are then two basic types of plastics. Their names are important as they affect the choice of plastics for particular jobs. The craft plastics are mostly **Thermoplastic** because they become soft when they are heated. The others are called **Thermosetting,** which means that they can be moulded and set by heating them up. Once they have been set they cannot be reheated to shape them again. These plastics are mostly used for things such as light fittings, switches, and crockery such as 'Melamine' ware.

All plastics are 'resins' and start life as 'monomers', which are mostly thick liquids. These are changed into 'polymers' by the

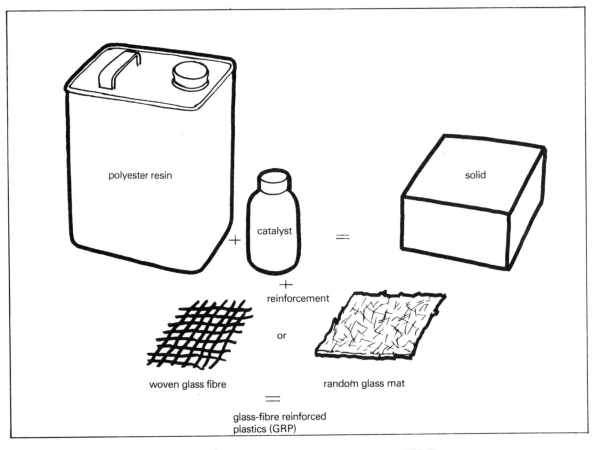

polyester resin + catalyst = solid

+

reinforcement

woven glass fibre   or   random glass mat

=

glass-fibre reinforced plastics (GRP)

addition of catalysts—materials which make the change occur without themselves taking part in the chemical reaction —and by using high temperatures and pressures in many cases. Most polymers are solids. The polymers we are most interested in as craft materials are **acrylic sheet** ('Perspex', 'Oroglas', 'Plexiglass' are all trade names for acrylic resins) and **polyester resins,** which come as a liquid monomer and catalyst. These are used for glass-fibre structures such as boats, dishes etc., for sculpture, to embed specimens for science, or just as beautiful objects. Lastly there are **epoxy resins,** which are either used for surface decorations as 'cold enamel' or as adhesives such as 'Araldite'.

Acrylic sheet can be cut, bent (when warmed) and glued using chemicals such as chloroform (which is toxic), acetone, or special adhesives, which are the best to use.

Safety

There are several safety hazards when you work with plastics of any kind. When you cut acrylic sheet wear your goggles because glass-like splinters can fly off. Never snap acrylic sheet for the same reason. Never burn plastics because most of them give off toxic fumes. Always have the room well ventilated when you work with plastics, especially polyester resins. If you ever get any of the chemicals on your skin wash it off immediately with water.

Perspex Mobile

You have done quite a lot of cutting, shaping and drilling of metals, and now you can find out how different, or how similar, Perspex will be when you cut, shape and drill it compared with the metals you have used. Before you start working with this material you must remember all the safety precautions for working with plastics which are on page 39.

A mobile is a decorative construction consisting basically of wires from which shapes are hung on threads. You can make a simple one by hanging shapes from each end of two wires, and suspending one of the wires under the other. The shapes move about in any breeze or draught in the room in which you hang the mobile. You can make the mobile more interesting by having some shapes bigger and therefore heavier than others, and then balancing the wires by hanging them not from their centres but at the centre of balance.

Try out a number of different shapes on paper first of all, and see how interesting you can make the mobile using four shapes and two wires only. The shapes should all follow the same 'theme' or subject for the best results.

To make your mobile

You will need: Pencil, coping saw, assorted files, 2 mm drill bit and hand drill, emery cloth, round-nosed pliers, 2 pieces of piano wire G.20 by 300 mm, 4 pieces of Perspex, reel of thread.

1   Draw out your shapes on to the paper which covers the Perspex.

2   Cut out the shapes with the coping saw and file to the lines you have drawn.

3   Smooth all the edges with emery cloth and if possible polish them.

4   Mark and drill a 2 mm hole near the top edge of each piece at the centre of balance.

5   Twist ends of wires into loops.

6   Join the shapes to the wires using the thread. Get the lengths looking right by trial and error. Find the balance point of each wire and make a 'kink' in it with the pliers. Join the wires together with thread. (Leave enough over to hang the mobile up with.)

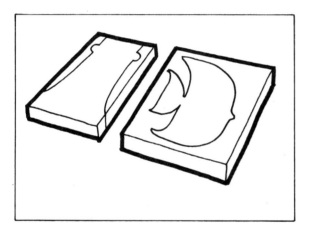

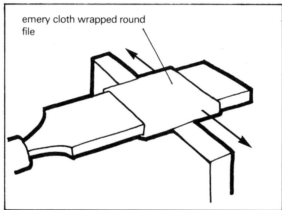

emery cloth wrapped round file

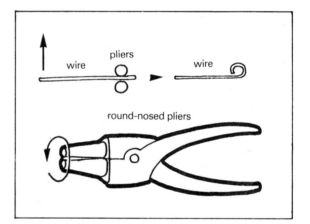

wire   pliers   wire

round-nosed pliers

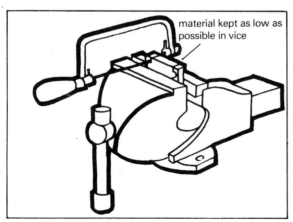

material kept as low as possible in vice

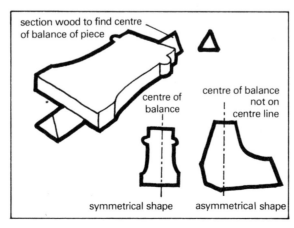

section wood to find centre of balance of piece

centre of balance

centre of balance not on centre line

symmetrical shape   asymmetrical shape

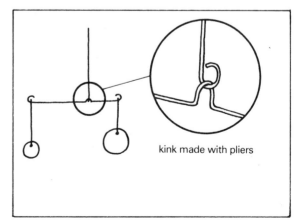

kink made with pliers

Glass Reinforced Plastics

As we have seen, plastic resins can be used as liquids to be poured into moulds. These moulded objects made from polyester resin are not very strong. It would not be very useful to make a car body from such a weak material and yet it can be done. By reinforcing the resin with fibres of glass we can produce a very strong, relatively lightweight material called glass fibre or **GRP** which means **Glass Reinforced Plastics.**

To make an object out of GRP we first have to prepare a mould. The mould must be a mirror image of the object we want, so we start by making a solid model of the object full size. This model is finished with a highly polished surface so that the mould will have a good finish as well. The mould is made of glass fibre by laying the material on to the wooden model which is called a **plug.** When the mould is set, it is removed from the plug. This is how glass fibre boats are made.

Polyester resin will stick to almost any surface, so we treat the plug and the mould with **release agents** to which the plastic cannot adhere. These agents are wax polish and a special release agent supplied by the manufacturers of the resins.

There are several stages to **'laying up'** glass fibre starting with the coat which will be the 'outside' or good side of the finished object or mould. This is done by mixing up a **gel-coat** resin with pigment (colour)

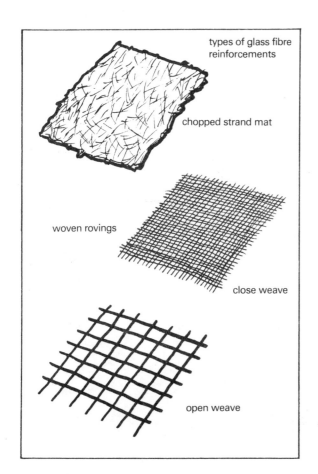

types of glass fibre reinforcements

chopped strand mat

woven rovings

close weave

open weave

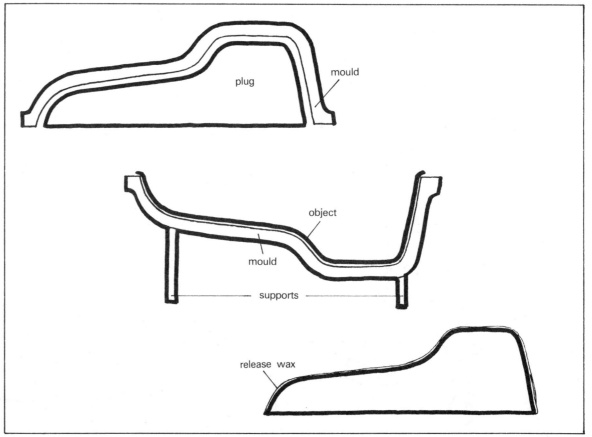

plug

mould

object

mould

supports

release wax

and catalyst, and painting this over the surface. It takes about half an hour to dry, which it does with a tacky surface. Next you must lay on the glass strands which are supplied in the form of a mat which you cut to shape before putting it on to the mould surface. Now you must mix up 'lay up' resin with its catalyst, and brush plenty of it into the mat until the glass fibres are completely covered. For strong structures you may have to put on more than one layer of glass mat. The resin is applied by pushing it into the mat with the end of the brush rather than painting it on because this 'stippling' action pushes the fibres together and forces out any air which might be trapped under the mat.

When the resin has set but not become hard you can trim the edges of the moulding with a sharp knife. This stage is called the 'green' stage. Once this stage is passed the resin sets very hard, and it is completely 'cured' after a few days.

All the tools you use should be cleaned as soon as you have finished using them. To remove the resin you must use acetone and then detergent.

When you work with these resins you should always have the room well ventilated and if possible wear a respirator. Protect your eyes with goggles and your hands with barrier cream and disposable gloves. If you get glass fibres under your skin they will be very painful.

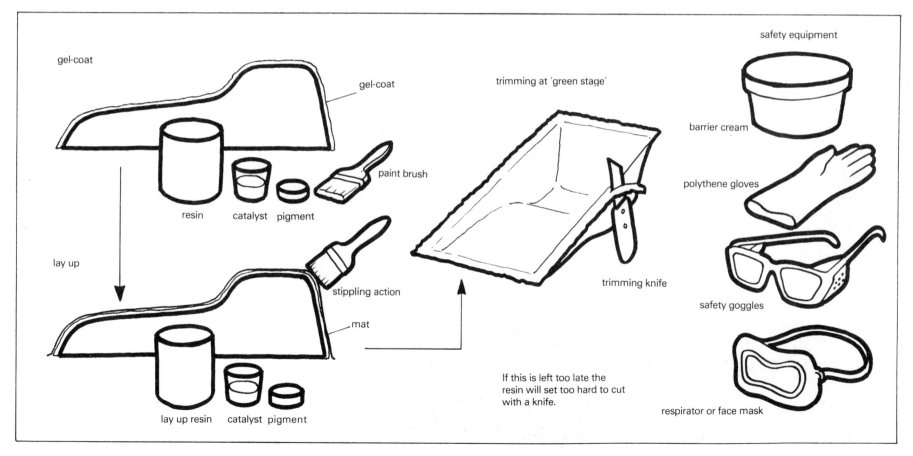

gel-coat

gel-coat

resin   catalyst   pigment

paint brush

lay up

stippling action

lay up resin   catalyst   pigment

mat

trimming at 'green stage'

trimming knife

If this is left too late the resin will set too hard to cut with a knife.

safety equipment

barrier cream

polythene gloves

safety goggles

respirator or face mask

GRP Dish

The manufacture of a glass fibre tank—applying the gel-coat.

In this job you are going to make a small container out of glass fibre. The choice of mould is fairly limited, but you can use any stainless steel or similar dish. When you have selected the one you want to reproduce you must decide, on the basis of what for and where it is to be used, which side is to be the 'good' side. If it is to be used for anything liquid or sticky then the inside should be smooth and the outside of the mould used. This will make it easier to wash up and it will be more hygenic. If it is to be mainly decorative then it might be better if the outside were smooth and the inside of the mould used. Your other design consideration is the colour you want to make it, and your choice will depend on the use to which your dish is to be put and the place where it is to be kept or displayed.

To make your dish

You will need: A container to use as a mould, release wax, release agent, gel coat resin, lay-up resin, catalyst, pigment paste, chopped strand glass mat, lay-up tissue, lay-up brush, acetone, trimming knife, wet-and-dry paper, newspaper, barrier cream, disposable gloves, goggles and respirator.

1 Apply two coats of release wax to the surface of the mould. Allow each coat to dry before putting on the next. Brush evenly with PVA release agent.

2 Mix gel-coat with pigment paste and catalyst. Brush on to mould. Wash brush.

3 Cut out the chopped strand mat and the tissue to fit the mould with a little over.

4 Mix lay-up resin, pigment and catalyst. Lay mat on to mould and stipple in plenty of resin. Repeat with a layer of tissue. Make sure that the surface is as smooth as possible when you have finished. Clean your brush.

5 When the green stage is reached trim the edge of the glass fibre with a sharp knife.

6 When the resin is completely cured release your dish from the mould. Smooth the edges with the wet-and-dry paper (used wet). Wash out the dish with plenty of detergent and water.

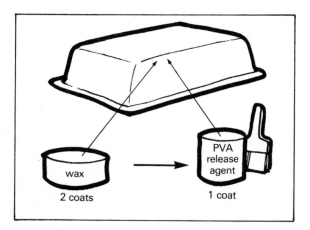

wax
2 coats

PVA release agent
1 coat

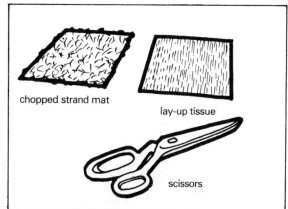

chopped strand mat

lay-up tissue

scissors

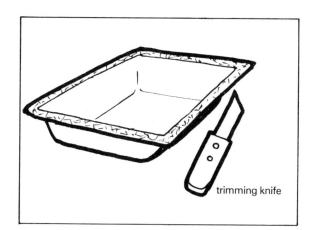

trimming knife

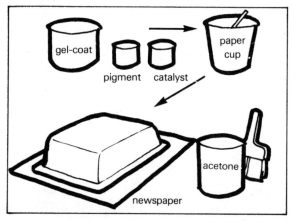

gel-coat

pigment   catalyst

paper cup

acetone

newspaper

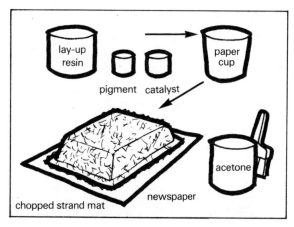

lay-up resin

pigment   catalyst

paper cup

acetone

chopped strand mat   newspaper

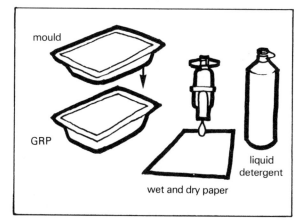

mould

GRP

wet and dry paper

liquid detergent

`Stained Glass' Decoration

One of the effects you can produce by colouring clear resin and then catalysing it is similar to transparent or translucent glass. You can use this effect to make a window decoration (with transparent pigments) or a Christmas tree decoration (with opaque colours). In either case the technique —the way you do it—is the same.

Polyester resins will not stick to paraffin wax, so you can make a mould from a block of this wax. By pouring resin into such a mould without using glass fibre you can cast a shape in solid plastic.

To make your decoration

You will need: A tobacco tin filled about two-thirds full with paraffin wax, a lino cutter with a narrow V blade, paper mixing cups, and sticks. Clear casting resin, catalyst, pigments, wet-and-dry paper.

1 Design your decoration so that it consists of areas of colour separated by 'bars' like a stained-glass window. Then cut the design into the wax with the lino cutter. Cut a border round the whole design about 3 mm in from the edge of the tin.

2 Mix clear resin and catalyst. Pour it on to your mould so that it fills the grooves and covers the whole of the wax to a depth of about 3 mm.

3 When the resin has set hard (about 3 hours) remove it from the mould.

4 Lightly roughen the areas to be coloured. Mix up some resin in different containers with different pigments. Catalyse them and carefully pour them into the areas you have prepared. Allow to harden completely.

5 Smooth the edges with wet-and-dry paper. In order to hang the decoration up you can fix a small loop of wire to the back with a drop of catalysed resin. Alternatively you could drill a small hole in the middle of the top edge.

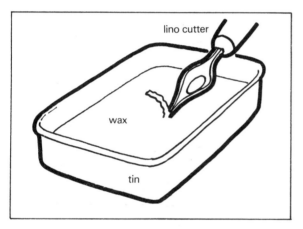

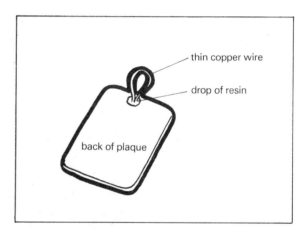

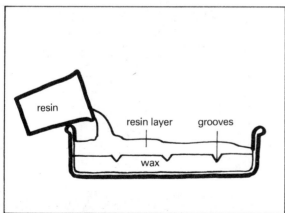

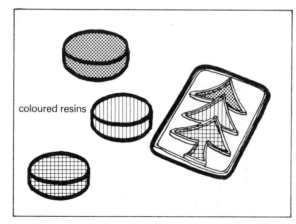

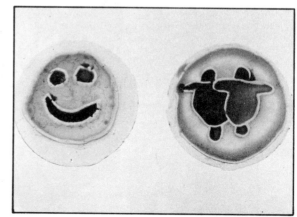

Cast Resin Paperweight

You have made a small object by pouring clear and coloured resin into a mould of wax. That casting was very small but now you are going to make a much larger casting from resin and you are going to put something in it. This is called embedding, and the technique is very similar to the other job using polyester resin. You will need to use a mould, but it will be deeper and must have a perfectly smooth surface. You cannot use a mould made of polystyrene because when you cast large

blocks of resin. a great deal of heat is produced by the chemical reaction. Special moulds made of glazed pottery or polythene are available but they are expensive. You can use a length of polythene drain or waste pipe for straight-sided castings. It is important to avoid undercuts on your mould, because anything that will prevent you from releasing your finished block from your mould will mean either the destruction of the mould, which is wasteful, or that you will have to throw away

the finished job!

Your choice of object for embedding is unlimited— from biological specimens to sea shells or bits of old clocks— so you should have no difficulty in choosing. The actual method is the same as any other resin casting job except that you must only mix and pour a small quantity at a time. This is because of the heat generated. If you have a very large block the heat will crack it.

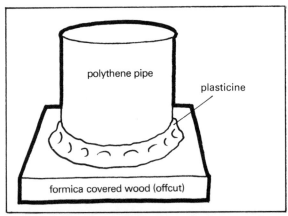

polythene pipe

plasticine

formica covered wood (offcut)

To make your casting

You will need: A mould, release wax and agent, mixing and measuring cups, casting resin, lay-up resin, pigment, catalyst, wet-and-dry paper, an object to be embedded, safety equipment, old newspapers.

1 Prepare your mould as you did for the dish.

2 Mix up enough casting resin and catalyst to make a layer about 5 mm deep and pour it into the mould. Let it harden— about 3 hours.

3 Repeat this pouring until you have as deep a layer as you need above the object. Remember that you are working upside down!

4 Pour a small quantity of resin into the mould and position the object upside-down on it. Pour on more resin to cover the object, but not more than about 10 mm.

5 Repeat the pouring of small layers until the object is covered by about 5 mm of resin.

6 For the final layer mix enough lay-up resin with opaque pigment and catalyst to make a layer between 5 mm and 10 mm deep. Set aside to cure for at least 12 hours.

7 Remove your paperweight from the mould and flatten the bottom with the wet-and-dry paper used wet. Polish all surfaces.

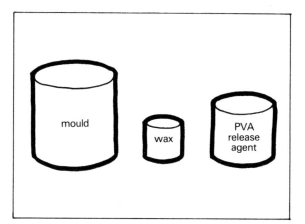

mould

wax

PVA release agent

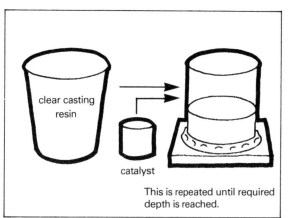

clear casting resin

catalyst

This is repeated until required depth is reached.

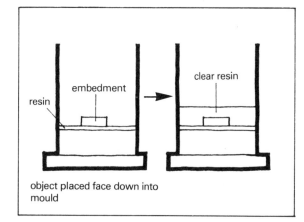

resin

embedment

clear resin

object placed face down into mould

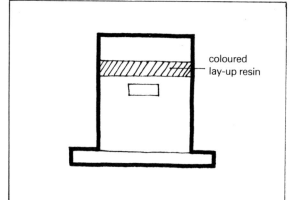

coloured lay-up resin

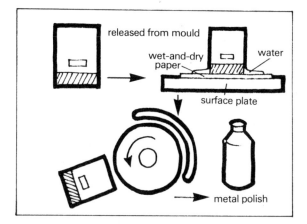

released from mould

wet-and-dry paper

water

surface plate

metal polish

Safety

Remember all your safety precautions when you work with polyester resins, Wear barrier cream, gloves, goggles and respirator. Protect the table or bench top with old newspapers. Ventilate the room well.

The Lathe

The **lathe** is the basic engineering machine tool and is probably the most widely used of all machines in factories, workshops, etc. It is used for turning cylindrical forms, in other words, it makes shapes like rods rather than balls. You can combine many sizes and forms of round section to make very complicated items using the lathe.

The lathe consists of a long **bed** with a **headstock** at one end and a **tailstock** at the other end. Between these two is the **saddle,** which can be moved along the bed. The tailstock can also be moved, but the headstock is fixed, and the **chuck**—the part which holds the work—is attached to it. The chuck is turned by an electric motor. A sharp cutting tool is attached to the saddle by means of a **tool-post.** This is usually fixed to the saddle by two 'slides', the **cross-slide,** which can be moved in and out across the bed, and the **top-slide** which can be moved along the bed. The top-slide is used for cutting along the metal either straight (which makes the metal narrower) or at an angle (which tapers the metal). The tailstock can be fitted either with a drill chuck like the drilling machine, or with a **centre** to support long thin pieces of metal which would otherwise flap about as you tried to cut them.

The lathe works by revolving the metal against the cutting tool. This is the opposite way round from bench work where we move the tool against the metal, but

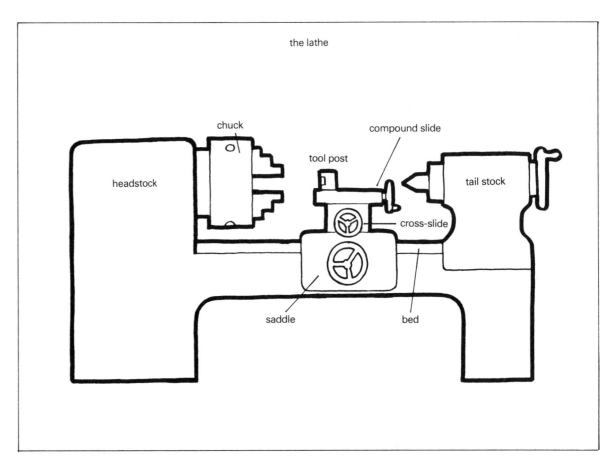

the lathe

headstock · chuck · tool post · compound slide · tail stock · cross-slide · saddle · bed

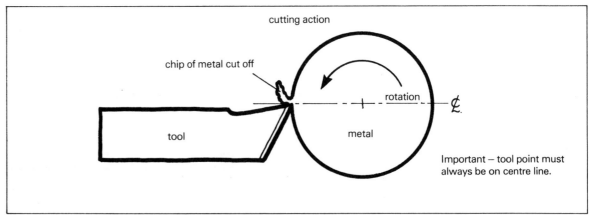

cutting action

chip of metal cut off

rotation · ₵

tool · metal

Important – tool point must always be on centre line.

50

the effect is just the same—the metal is shaped by the tool.

There are two main operations for which the lathe is used. These are called **facing** and **turning.** To **face** a piece of metal in the lathe you set it into the chuck which you do up tightly on to the metal. You set the machine going and move the tool across the end surface (or face) of the metal, flattening it and removing any un-evenness. To **turn** the metal you move the tool along the metal either with the saddle or the top slide so that you reduce its diameter. There are many variations to those two basic movements depending on the angle or shape of the tool or the angle at which the compound slide (the name for an adjustable top-slide) is set, but the movements are still either along or across the work.

By cutting along the metal for a short distance we can produce steps in the metal, and by cutting 'across' the metal, even if not at the end, with a narrow tool we can make grooves in it.

By using the tailstock with a drill chuck in it we can use the lathe as an accurate drilling machine. Instead of using a centre punch to mark the middle of the hole we use a special drill called a centre drill.

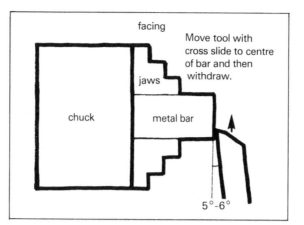

facing

Move tool with cross slide to centre of bar and then withdraw.

chuck

jaws

metal bar

5°-6°

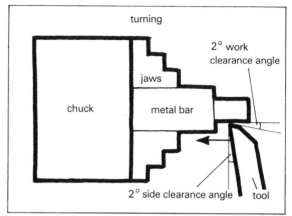

turning

2° work clearance angle

chuck

jaws

metal bar

2° side clearance angle

tool

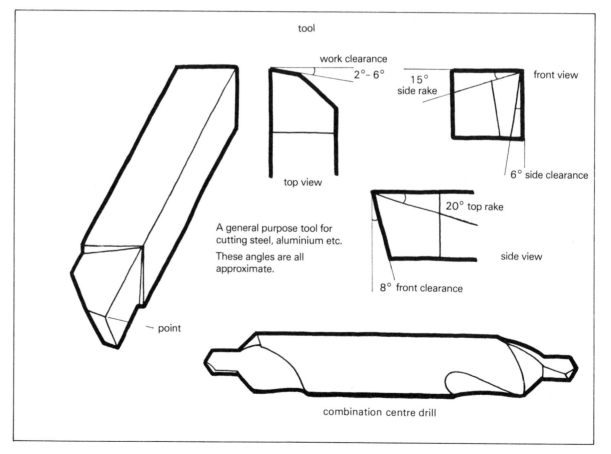

tool

work clearance 2°- 6°

15° side rake

front view

6° side clearance

top view

20° top rake

8° front clearance

side view

A general purpose tool for cutting steel, aluminium etc. These angles are all approximate.

point

combination centre drill

Small Turned Candle Holder

By using the actions of turning and facing on the lathe you can produce a very attractive and unusual candle holder to take a flower taper type of candle. When designing your candle holder try to restrict yourself to a finished size of 25 mm diameter and about 50 mm high. You can experiment on paper with shapes made up of steps and/or grooves, but you must bear in mind that there will be a hole about 6 mm diameter through the middle to a depth of about 15 mm, and also that a candle is a tall object and so will need as wide a base as possible to prevent it from toppling over.

To make your candle holder

You will need: A length of aluminium bar 25 mm diameter by well over 60 mm long, facing, turning and grooving tools, tail-stock chuck, centre drill, 6 mm drill, hacksaw, cutting oil, goggles for your eyes.

1 Fit the metal into the chuck securely with at least 55 mm protruding. Set the facing tool correctly and face the end of the bar.
2 Now cut your steps into the metal. Do not cut too deeply where the hole is to be drilled. To turn the metal you will need to change the tool from a facing to a turning tool.
3 If you want to cut grooves you must now change tools again to a grooving tool.

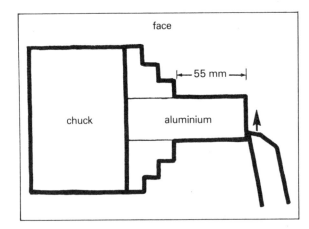

face

chuck   aluminium

|←— 55 mm —→|

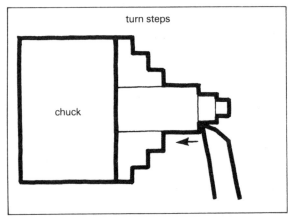

turn steps

chuck

When you have set it you use it by moving it into the metal with the cross-slide. Do not operate the top-slide or the saddle when the grooving tool is cutting.

Safety

Always use cutting oil when cutting aluminium on the lathe. (Paraffin is a suitable alternative to soluble oil.) Your teacher will show you the safe way to apply it with a brush.

4   Remove the cutting tools from the tool post. Fit the tailstock chuck. Put the centre drill into the tailstock chuck. Move the tailstock close to the work. Drill the end of the bar with the tip of the centre drill.

5   Change the centre drill for the 6 mm drill bit. Drill the end of the bar to a depth of about 15 mm.

6   Now remove the bar from the chuck and saw off the candle holder about 55 mm from the end. (You will not be able to saw perfectly straight, and that is why you should allow 5 mm extra.)

7   Replace the candle holder in the chuck but this time with the sawn end outwards. Use the facing tool to smooth the end of the candle holder until it is perfectly flat.

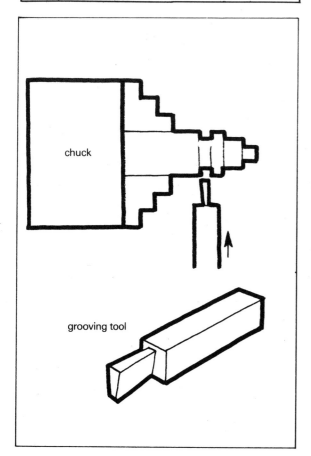

chuck

grooving tool

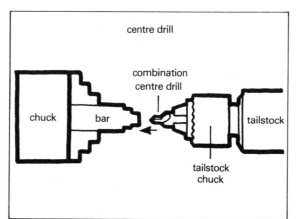

centre drill

combination centre drill

chuck   bar   tailstock

tailstock chuck

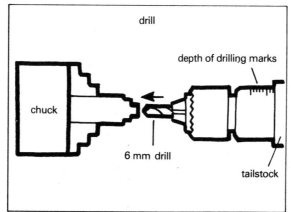

drill

depth of drilling marks

chuck

6 mm drill

tailstock

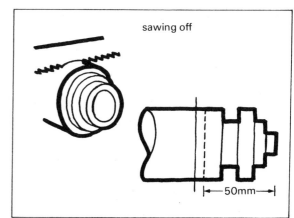

sawing off

50mm

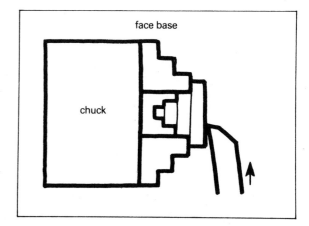

face base

chuck

Surface Decoration

Enamelling

There are several ways of permanently decorating the surface of a piece of metal. Some of these ways are also used to give the surface a protective covering so that it will not go dull. One method is called **enamelling.** This can be done in many ways with two sorts of material. The traditional way is to fuse (melt) coloured glass powder on to the surface of a piece of metal in a special oven called a **kiln.** Another form of enamelling using heat is called **low-temperature enamelling.** This uses powdered plastics, and instead of a kiln it needs only a candle under a wire gauze stand.

Enamelling by either of these methods is basically the same. A metal **blank** (usually copper) is cleaned and then painted with a special gum. Now you sprinkle the coloured glass powder evenly over the surface of the blank. Put the blank on top of the kiln to dry the gum. When this is done you must put the blank into the hot kiln (about 900° C) for no more than 1½ minutes. Take the blank out and let it cool. The blank is handled with a tool called a **spatula.** When the blank is cool you must re-cover it with enamel powder and then 'fire' it again for about 2 minutes. When it has cooled this time you will find that it has a smooth, shining, coloured surface.

There are several different ways of enamelling. They are called 'Sgraffito', 'Cloisonné', and 'Champlevé'. **Sgraffito**

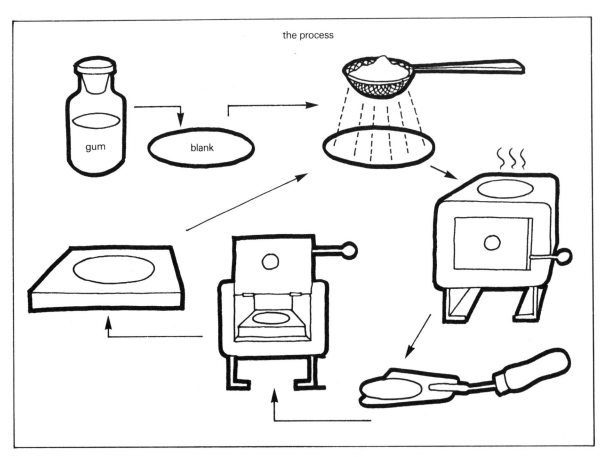

the process

gum · blank

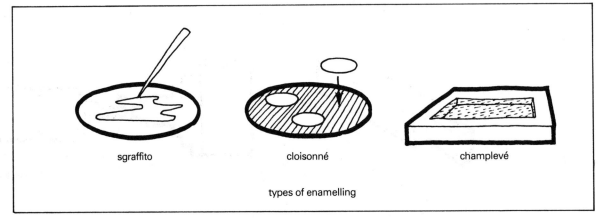

sgraffito · cloisonné · champlevé

types of enamelling

54

means that you fire one colour on to the blank and then sprinkle a second colour on top. Before you fire this colour you scratch a design in the powder with a fine-pointed tool. After firing you will find that the design appears as a line of the original colour against a background of the second colour. If you want to make designs more like pictures with larger areas of colour you can use **cloisonné**. This means making shapes out of thin copper wire. When you fire the blank the first time you use an enamel called a flux which is usually clear glass powder. Once this has cooled you arrange the pieces of wire on the surface. You now fill the areas formed by the wires with the colours of enamel that you have chosen. When you have filled all the areas you fire the blank for the second time. The wires are now held in place by the melting enamel and when the blank has cooled they are fixed into their positions. In **champlevé** enamelling you prepare the blank by making some areas of it lower than others to form small depressions into which the enamels can be fired. This can be done by hammering or etching (see below). You then treat the blank as if it was a plain one, but you must do each stage to all the areas at the same time.

Each of these techniques can also be carried out, but much more simply though not so quickly, with **cold enamels** which are a type of casting resin plastic material. In this case heat is not needed nor is a second coat, except for sgraffito enamelling.

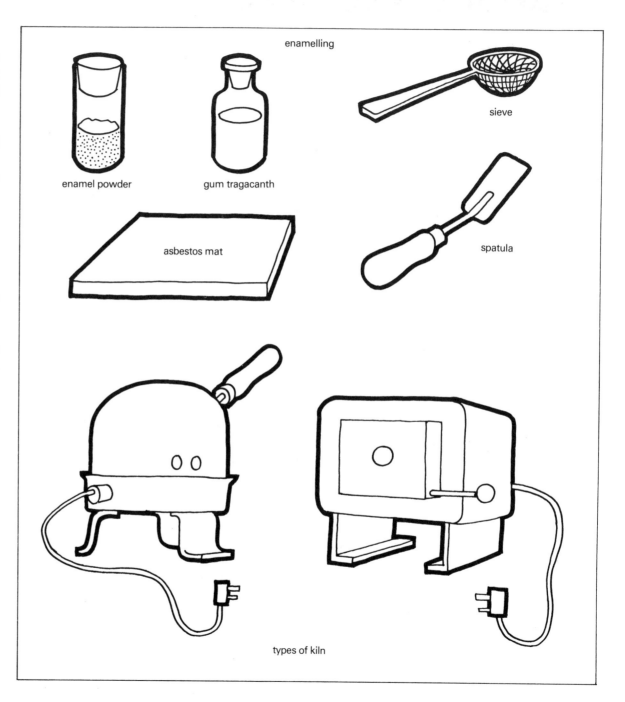

enamelling

enamel powder

gum tragacanth

sieve

asbestos mat

spatula

types of kiln

Surface Decoration

Dip coating

Another plastic coating treatment is called **dip coating**. This is a purely protective treatment for steel which covers the metal completely with coloured plastic. It is used for making things such as supermarket baskets out of steel rod, and prevents rusting while at the same time making the article more attractive. It is also used for steel furniture such as chair and table frames. The plastic is used in the form of a powder kept in a **fluid-bed** tank. This is a box with a porous bottom. Air is blown through the bottom of the tank and the powder then behaves as if it were a liquid. If you then put steel heated to about 230°C into the tank the plastic will stick evenly to the surface. When you take the steel out and reheat it the plastic fuses into a smooth covering. You can use this to coat the handles of pliers or small saws.

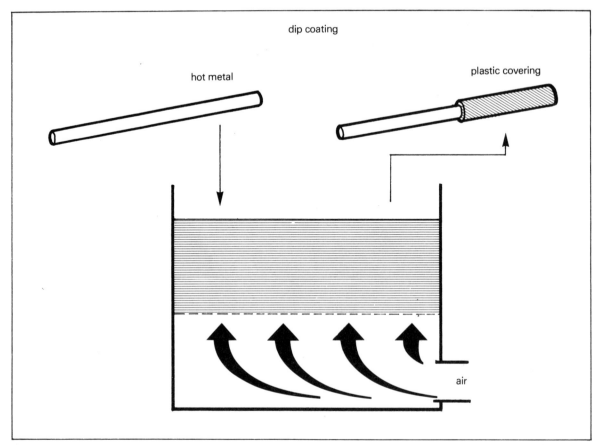

dip coating

hot metal

plastic covering

air

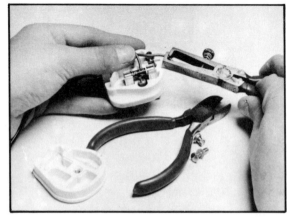

Etching

Another form of decorative treatment is called **etching**. This means that you remove part of the surface of the metal. You can do this by covering some parts of the surface with a special paint (which you take off later) called an **etch-resist**. Then you put the metal into a chemical which dissolves the parts which have not been painted. Suitable chemicals are dilute nitric acid (which is not very safe) or ferric chloride which is safer than the acid and works more slowly. If you try to etch metal too fast you get very poor results. This is a case of patience being the key to success! The best metal for etching in school is one which contains copper (brass or gilding metal).

All these methods of surface decoration can be used on a wide variety of projects that you can do.

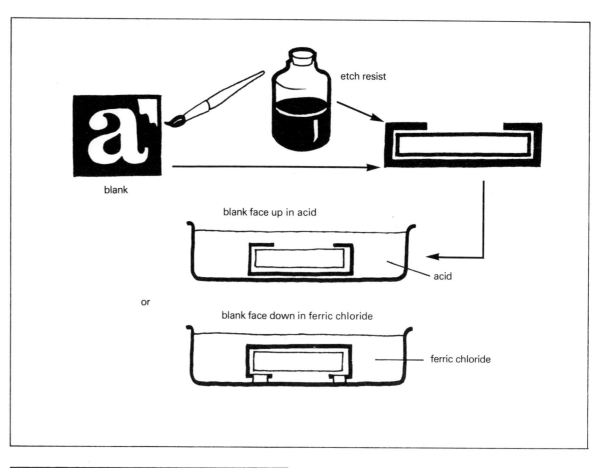

etch resist

blank

blank face up in acid

acid

or

blank face down in ferric chloride

ferric chloride

Etching is used to produce some 'printed' circuits, as in this transistor radio.

Enamelled Pendant

To make an enamelled pendant you will have to start by making several designs. You could look at natural forms such as leaves or at geometric shapes to get some ideas. To make patterns on the enamel you can mask off areas with paper (a method called **stencilling**), or you can use any of the techniques described in the section about surface decoration on page 54.

To make your pendant

You will need: A metal blank (copper about 1 mm thick) in which you have drilled a small hole near one edge, coloured enamel powders, a sieve, gum tragacanth, a paint brush, emery cloth, asbestos mat, spatula, clean paper.

1 Cut the blank to shape. Finish the edges. Clean the surface with emery cloth. Do not touch it with your fingers once it is cleaned.

2 Paint a thin layer of gum on to the blank. Lift the blank on to a clean piece of paper.

3 Sprinkle the first coat of enamel powder on to the blank. Make sure that the edges are well covered.

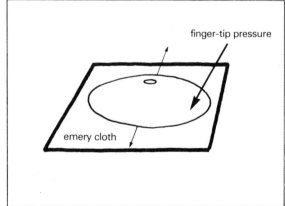

finger-tip pressure

emery cloth

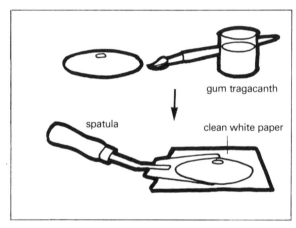

gum tragacanth

spatula

clean white paper

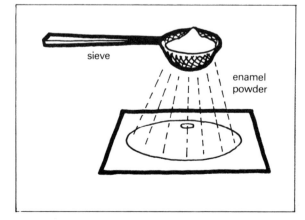

sieve

enamel powder

4   Put the blank on top of the hot kiln for the gum to dry. Now lift the blank into the kiln and fire it for 1½ minutes only. Lift it out on to the asbestos mat to cool.

5   At this stage, once the blank is cool, you can carry out the sgraffito, cloisonné, champlevé or stencil methods of enamelling. The second firing, if it is the last, can be for 2 to 3 minutes to achieve a very smooth surface. If you are going to do more than one more firing then all coats except the last should only be fired for 1½ minutes.

6   After the last firing you must let the blank become absolutely cold. When it is cold you can clean the back with emery cloth until all the black 'fire scale' has been removed. Carefully clean up the edges with emery cloth but do not touch the enamelled surface with the cloth because it is easily scratched.

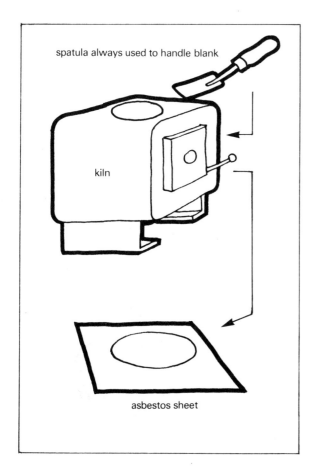

spatula always used to handle blank

kiln

asbestos sheet

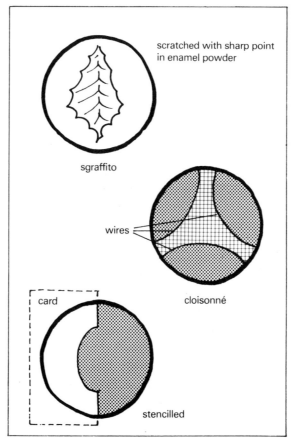

scratched with sharp point in enamel powder

sgraffito

wires

cloisonné

card

stencilled

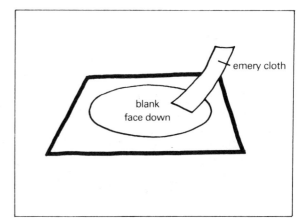

emery cloth

blank
face down

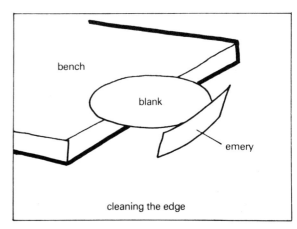

bench

blank

emery

cleaning the edge

Brass Etching

Now that you have had some experience of cutting and shaping metals to give an accurate finish you can turn your attention to the possible uses of small rectangular tags of metal with decorated surfaces. Think of a use for a piece about 50 mm wide and any length. The point of this job is that you are going to work on the surface of the metal to produce an effect of two or more different levels. You could make a name plate (not very exciting), or another pendant, or a key tag, or a belt buckle, which has many possibilities.

Whatever you choose to make, after you have worked out the right size for it (What is it for? Where is it to be used? What is the best size to do the job properly?) cut out your metal and finish the edges and angles accurately. The design you put on the front is again entirely up to you, but it must fit the purpose of the job and it must also be attractive to look at. If you do decide to make a belt buckle you will also have to work out how it is to be fixed to, and hold, your belt!

To make your piece

You will need: A brass rectangle about 2 mm thick, files, emery cloth, polisher, liquid detergent, a small artist's paintbrush, cellulose paint to use as stop-out varnish (even nail varnish will do for this!), acetone (to clean the brush), Ferric Chloride solution, an etch bath (a small photographic dish is ideal).

1 Prepare your metal with perfectly straight edges and right-angle corners. Draw-file the edges and polish the blank all over. It must be completely 'finished', because the etching is the last stage of manufacture. If you are making a buckle with slots, cut them now. If any drilling or soldering has to be done it must be completed before polishing.

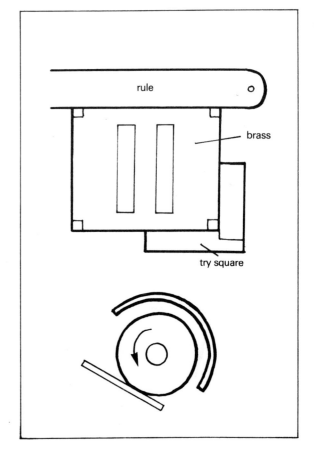

rule

brass

try square

2 Carefully clean the surface of the metal with a strong solution of liquid detergent. This removes any grease which would prevent the resist from sticking or the etchant from doing its job.

3 When the metal is dry, carefully paint with the stop-out varnish the areas you do not want removed. Do not touch the metal with your fingers. Allow the varnish to dry completely.

4 Paint the back of the metal (and the edges) with varnish. Allow to dry.

5 Put the blank face down into the etch bath. Leave it there for a few days.

6 When the etching is complete, remove it from the bath and wash it, and your hands, with plenty of cold water. You can clean off the varnish with acetone and polish the metal with liquid metal polish to bring back the shine.

7 The process you have now done is the simplest form of etching. If you want to make a more interesting piece you can etch on several levels. If you want to do this you now paint out the metal again but this time you expose more of the surface to the etchant. The parts already etched will be cut deeper, but the new parts will not be cut so deeply and will give a layered effect. This can be repeated several times until the required design has been built up.

washing-up liquid

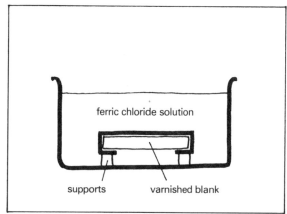

ferric chloride solution

supports   varnished blank

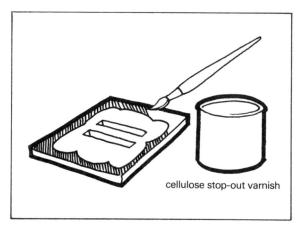

cellulose stop-out varnish

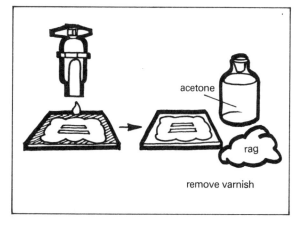

acetone

rag

remove varnish

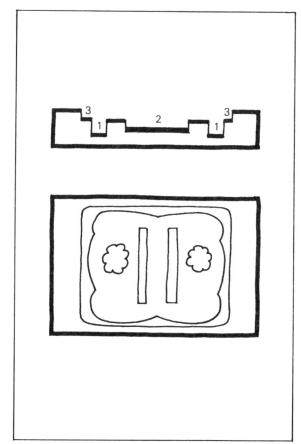

Forming Perspex

Acrylic sheet can be formed into complex shapes by heating it in an oven and then bending or pressing it on to a **former**. A former is a shaped piece of wood or other material, the shape being the one you want the Perspex to have after you have finished the job.

Simple bends can be made very easily by using a strip heater made from some Nichrome wire stretched between two supports. If you connect 12 volts D.C. or A.C. across the wire it becomes red hot and gives off enough heat to soften acrylic sheet in a few minutes. This method is quite safe electrically, and so long as you do not touch the hot wire you will also be safe. You should only heat the area you want to bend (slowly so as not to scorch the surface of the plastic) until it becomes soft and floppy. You may now bend it to any angle. To fix the bend just cool it under a cold tap.

To make complex shapes on a former you have to heat the sheet in an oven until it is soft and pliable. When it is ready you press it between the two shaped halves of the former until it is cool. In both methods the heating and shaping are the last operations you perform; all cutting, filing and polishing must be done first.

Acrylic sheet softens at about 120°C.

Safety
Always work with hot Acrylic in well-ventilated conditions. The fumes can be toxic.

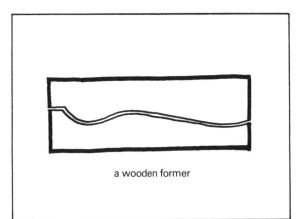

a wooden former

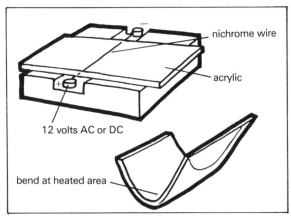

nichrome wire

acrylic

12 volts AC or DC

bend at heated area

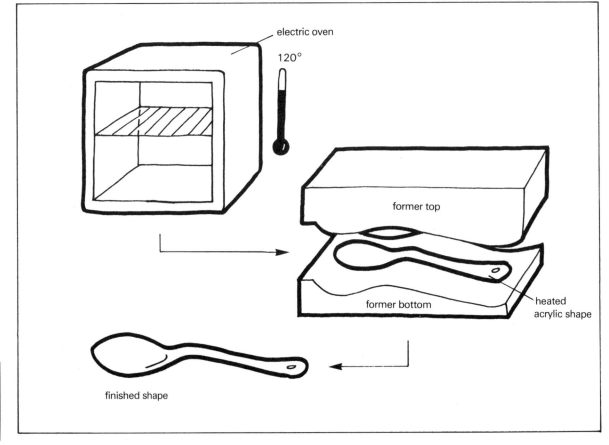

electric oven

120°

former top

former bottom

heated acrylic shape

finished shape

Egg Holder

You are now going to have the opportunity to decide on the best way to do a job without being given any detailed instructions. The only restrictions are the size of the piece of material you will be given and the stipulation that you must form it only by bending and/or cutting it into no more than two pieces. You may shape the material by sawing or filing as you see fit in order to hold an egg.

The most important part of this job is the design stage, and you must think very hard indeed about the meaning of all the terms used up to now in the sections on plastics, design, and the use of tools and processes. You must decide what the various functions of an egg holder are, and the various conditions of heat, moisture and physical pressure that it will have to put up with. You must also consider the aesthetic problems of the use of an egg holder.

To make your egg holder you will need any tools you think necessary. List them on a piece of paper. You will also need adhesive, if your design calls for it, and a piece of acrylic sheet 100 mm long by 50 mm wide by 3 mm thick.

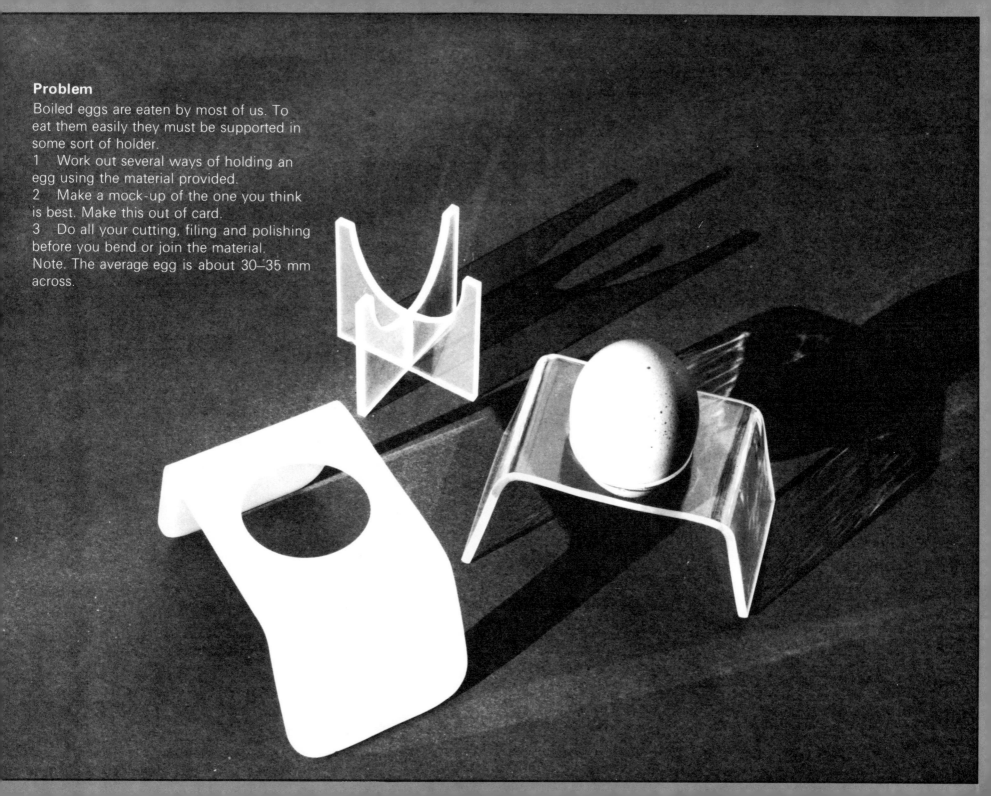

Problem

Boiled eggs are eaten by most of us. To eat them easily they must be supported in some sort of holder.

1   Work out several ways of holding an egg using the material provided.

2   Make a mock-up of the one you think is best. Make this out of card.

3   Do all your cutting, filing and polishing before you bend or join the material.

Note. The average egg is about 30–35 mm across.

Working with the Lathe

Parting off

Parting off is the term used in lathe work to mean cutting off to length. To do this we use a special lathe tool, similar to the tool used to cut the grooves in your candle holder. You should set the tool in the tool post so that it is exactly at right angles to the work to be cut off. Measure from the end of the work to the edge of the tool the amount you want to cut off. Now you start the lathe and feed the tool into the work using the cross-slide. You must take great care when you do this. It may be necessary to take the tool out of the work from time to time, especially if you are cutting aluminium, to prevent metal clogging the cutting edge. Except when you part off brass you should keep the work well lubricated and cooled with the correct cutting fluid.

You will find that even though the work is revolving at speed, when the tool cuts through the metal, the cut piece will not fly off but drop into the bed of the machine. It will be very hot indeed, so let it cool down for a few minutes before you try to pick it up.

Safety
Always wear your goggles and keep any guards on the machine in place when you part off.

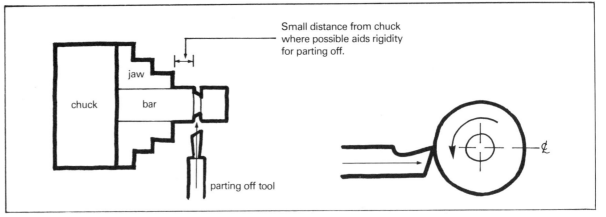

Small distance from chuck where possible aids rigidity for parting off.

chuck   jaw   bar

parting off tool

Operating the lathe. In the school workshop goggles would of course be worn.

Taper turning

If you want to form a point on the end of a piece of rod or bar you can do this with the lathe by means of a process called **taper turning**. This means that you are going to cut the metal at an angle as it revolves in the lathe.

To do this you use an ordinary turning tool in the tool post. To set the machine to cut an angle you must move the compound slide. On your lathe there will be a screw or nut holding the compound slide in its position, and a protractor scale showing the angle at which this slide is set. If you loosen this nut you will be able to turn the whole of the compound slide to the angle you want and then tighten the nut to hold the slide in that position. In order to work out the angle you need to set the slide to, you have to know the 'included' angle of the point. The slide angle will be half this because, as the work revolves in the lathe you are cutting the angle on 'both sides of the work at once' thus doubling the angle the tool cuts at.

Callipers

Callipers are tools used for measuring the thickness of materials or objects. There are two sorts of callipers, inside and outside. The inside one measures the insides of holes or 'gaps', and the outside one measures across any two surfaces which are parallel. They both consist of two legs joined at the top so that they can be opened up or closed together. The ends are bent to touch the object being measured. You use them by opening or closing the legs so that both touch the object and then measuring the gap between them with a rule.

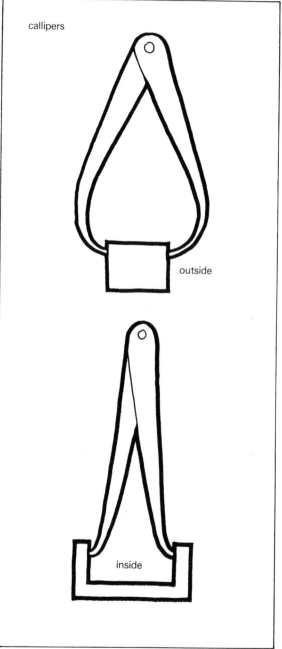

callipers

outside

inside

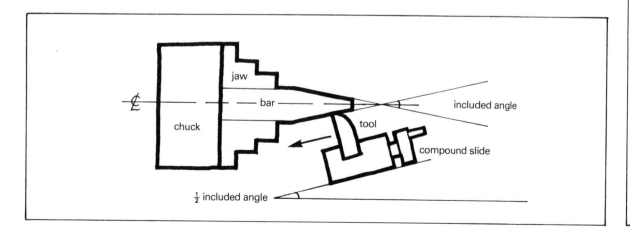

jaw

bar

included angle

chuck

tool

compound slide

½ included angle

Small Board Games

There are many small board games, or games played on paper, that you can make into very nice little board and peg games with a little imagination. Games like noughts and crosses or 'Nine Man Morris' and many others can be made by drilling holes into a piece of flat material and making pegs to fit the holes.

Start this project by finding out about a number of such games (and there are literally hundreds to choose from) and then use the experience you have of technique and materials to design a game using metal pegs and a plastics board. The pieces will probably have to be designed so that you can tell some of them apart. Do this by shape, decoration or colour.

Keep the size of your game as small as is practical, but where possible within a 90 mm square. The fewer pegs your game needs the less material and time it will take to make, and so the cheaper it will be. This is an important design consideration in industry, so you should now start to think about cost as an integral part of the design problem.

To make your game

You will need: Acrylic sheet 3 mm thick, metal rod, saws, files, lathe, drills and polisher.

1 Mark out, cut out, drill, finish and polish the board.

2 Put your rod into the lathe chuck and face the end.

3 Turn the step on the end to fit the holes in the board. Use callipers to measure this as you work. Stop the lathe before trying to use the callipers.

4 Part off to the right length. Shape the other end if necessary to tell the pieces apart.

5 Repeat the turning operations until you have enough pieces.

6 Polish the pegs.

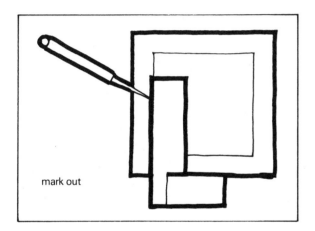

mark out

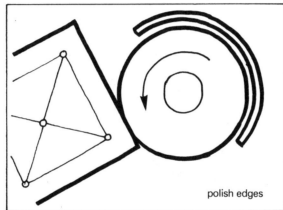

polish edges

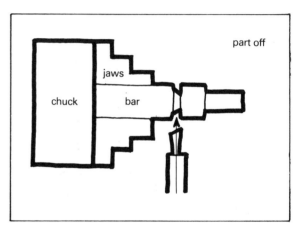

part off

chuck

jaws

bar

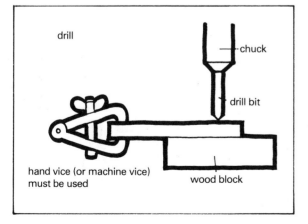

drill

chuck

drill bit

hand vice (or machine vice) must be used

wood block

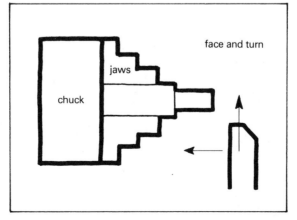

face and turn

chuck

jaws

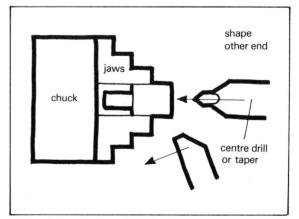

shape other end

chuck

jaws

centre drill or taper

Top Dice

By making spinning tops from six-sided metal bar you can make either dice or a cricket game. The important feature of spinning tops is that they must be properly balanced and so it is essential to make them accurately on a lathe.

You may be able to think of other games that tops can be used for besides dice and 'How's That!'

To make your top

You will need: A length of hexagonal brass or steel bar, 12.5 mm across flats, a facing and turning tool, a parting off tool, outside callipers, letter and number stamps.

(Stamps are used like a centre punch, but instead of a point they are made with the ends cut into the shape of a letter, a number or even a decorative pattern.)

1   Put the bar into the lathe chuck, holding it across flats.
2   Set the callipers to 5 mm. Turn the bar to a diameter of 5 mm for a length of 12.5 mm.
3   Part off the bar to a length of 30 mm.

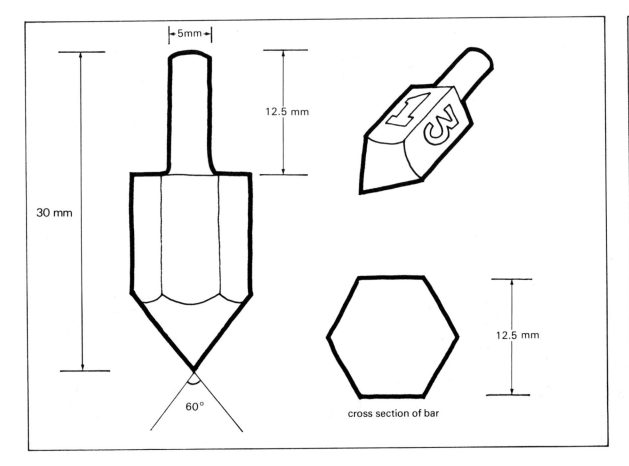

cross section of bar

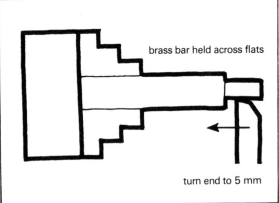

brass bar held across flats

turn end to 5 mm

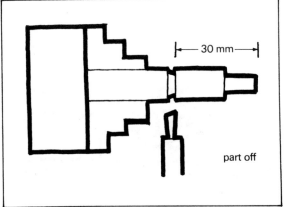

part off

4 Set the compound slide to 30°
5 Take the piece of bar and put it into the chuck, holding it by the turned end.
6 Turn this end to a 60° point.

7 Take the metal out of the chuck and stamp numbers from 1–6 on the faces. For dice the opposite sides must always add up to 7. For a cricket game see the drawing.

8 Flatten the stamped faces with emery cloth.

If you are making the cricket game you will need to make two tops.

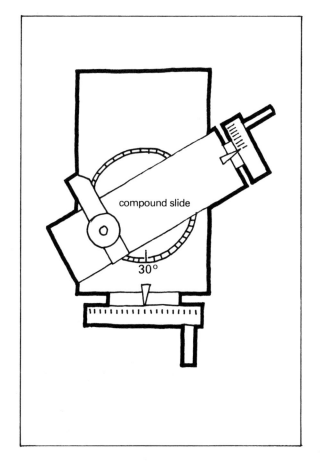

compound slide

30°

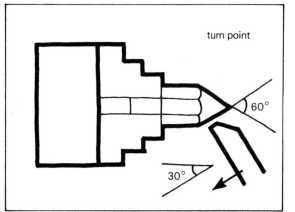

turn point

60°

30°

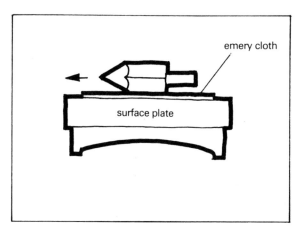

emery cloth

surface plate

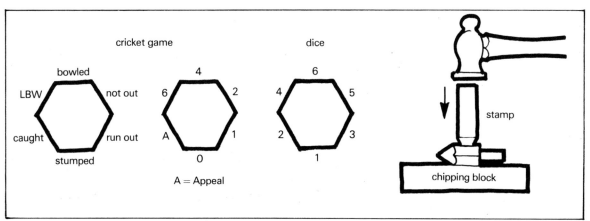

cricket game

bowled
LBW   not out
caught   run out
stumped

dice

4
6   2
A   1
0

6
4   5
2   3
1

A = Appeal

stamp

chipping block

Casting Metal

Just as you can pour liquid plastic into a mould to make complex objects so you can pour liquid (molten) metal into a mould. In the case of metals the moulds are made of sand, compacted round a pattern which you remove to leave a space which can be filled with metal through holes cut into the sand.

Patterns can be made from wood, which makes accurate, reusable forms, or from polystyrene foam (like ceiling tiles), which makes very complicated forms if necessary but can only be used once.

Whichever type of pattern you choose the process is similar. You put the pattern into a pair of boxes, called the **cope** and the **drag**, and then you ram sand round it with a wooden peg. In the case of wooden patterns you fill the boxes separately, the drag first and then the cope, so that they can be taken apart to remove the pattern.

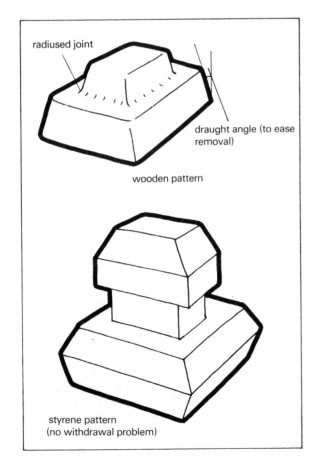

radiused joint

draught angle (to ease removal)

wooden pattern

styrene pattern
(no withdrawal problem)

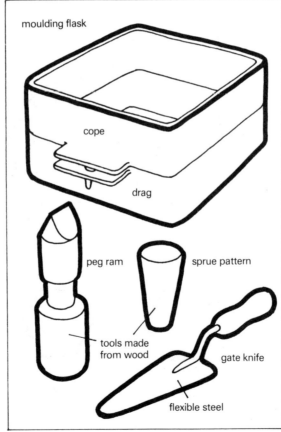

moulding flask

cope

drag

peg ram

sprue pattern

tools made from wood

gate knife

flexible steel

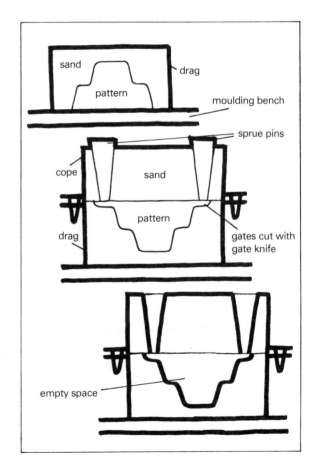

sand

drag

pattern

moulding bench

sprue pins

cope

sand

drag

pattern

gates cut with gate knife

empty space

When the boxes are full you cut holes down to the pattern through the sand for the metal to be poured into. If you use a polystyrene pattern you leave it in the sand because the molten metal will vapourise the plastic leaving the empty space to be filled.

When the metal has been melted in the furnace you pour it in one continuous operation into one of the holes in the sand, called the **runner**. You go on pouring until metal appears at the top of the other hole, the **riser**. This means that the space in the sand is now full of metal.

You must now leave the metal to harden, which takes about half an hour, and then you can dig the finished casting out of the sand. The casting will still be very hot and you must handle it with tongs until it is cool. It will also be attached to solid pieces of metal which were the runner and riser where the metal was poured in. These have to be cut off and the casting cleaned up to the required finish. This cleaning up operation is called **fettling**.

Making a polystyrene pattern is very simple. You can cut and shape the material with a heated wire or a broken saw blade heated in a bunsen flame. You can also cut it with a sharp knife. If you rub over the surface with glass paper you can produce a decorative texture which will be repeated in the metal when the pattern is cast.

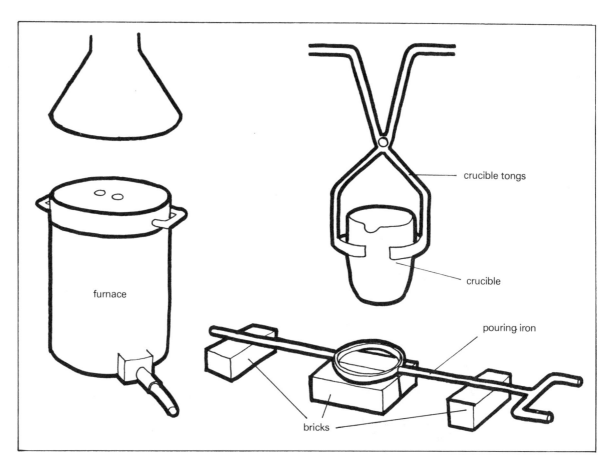

furnace

crucible tongs

crucible

pouring iron

bricks

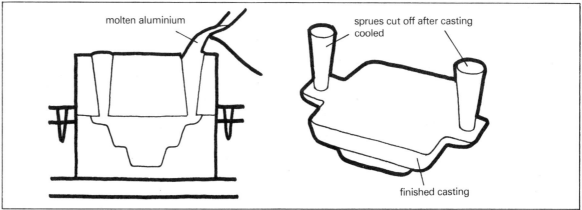

molten aluminium

sprues cut off after casting cooled

finished casting

Cast Block

for a paperweight, lamp base or table sculpture

You can use a block of polystyrene foam as a pattern for casting any number of decorative or useful items. If you like things such as paperweights or table sculptures in your home you can experiment with these, or you can turn them into a table lamp base simply by drilling a hole to take a lamp holder and a length of wire.

The metal you will use for your casting will be aluminium alloy LM4 because it melts easily and at a low enough temperature for a small school furnace to cope with. If you are going to make only a very small piece you can melt enough aluminium using the gas/air blow torch on the brazing hearth. When you are designing your object, try to concentrate on the texture of the surface you can produce. This is an area of decorative technique which is well suited to casting.

To make your object

You will need: Hot wire cutters and old hacksaw blades, a block of polystyrene 100 mm by 100 mm by 100 mm, casting sand, moulding boxes, moulding tools, aluminium alloy LM4, small furnace.

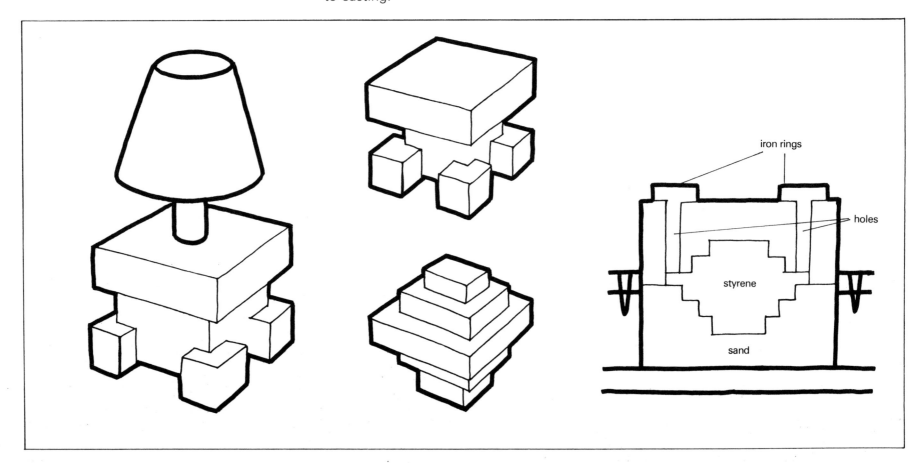

iron rings

holes

styrene

sand

74

1   Cut, shape and texture your polystyrene block.

2   Fit together the cope and drag and fill to a depth of about 50 mm with sand.

3   Put your pattern onto this bed of sand and fill the boxes with more sand, ramming it down layer by layer until the boxes are full.

4   With a piece of steel pipe cut two holes into the sand each side of the block. The holes should expose a small part of the pattern.

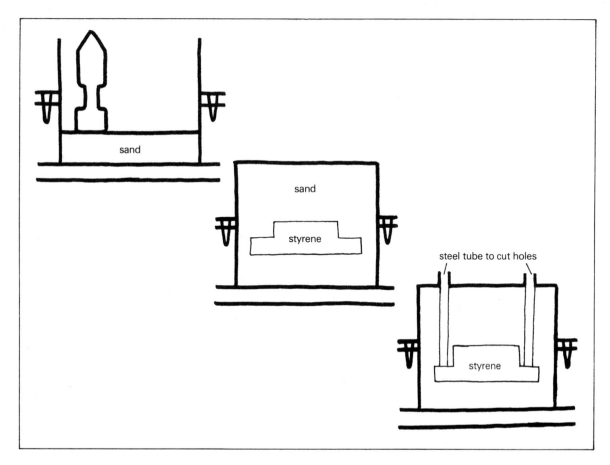

sand

sand

styrene

steel tube to cut holes

styrene

Important safety note.
When you are working with molten metals and furnaces it is essential that you do nothing without your teacher telling you directly to do it. You must always wear the protective clothing necessary for this process, namely safety goggles, leather apron, heat resistant gloves.

Never allow any water to come into contact with molten metal because it turns instantly into steam and becomes an explosive mixture. Always move slowly and with great care near casting activities. Never leave anything on the floor where it may trip you, or another person. Always make certain that the room is well ventilated and that respirators are available for use when you cast from polystyrene patterns because they give off poisonous fumes.

5   Move your boxes to the casting floor. Arrange the casting tools and **with the help of your teacher and no one else** pour molten metal into your mould.

6   After about half an hour dig out your casting and fettle it when it is cold.

Chasing

Chasing is a method of decorating sheet metal using small punches, straight, curved and patterned, which you hit with a special wide-faced hammer called a **repoussé hammer**. The action of enclosing an area of metal with a line stamped into its surface raises the area you have surrounded. By using only a small straight punch and a small curved one, you can achieve most of the intricate forms which were used in the periods of decorative design such as the Art Nouveau period at the end of the last century and the beginning of this.

To chase a panel or a shallow dished form you can lay the metal on to a thick pad of newspaper. This takes the place of a stake. Professionals use a board or iron bowl filled with pitch, but this is a more difficult way of doing this type of work. Another reason for using newspaper is that it is free, always a useful consideration! Newspaper is resilient and will move to a limited degree under the action of the punches. If you wanted to decorate a deep object you would have to use pitch as newsprint cannot be poured into deep vessels!

The punches are very easy to make using high carbon steel such as silver steel or hexagonal tool steel. You can use chased metal for small pieces of jewellery, or large panels such as decorated box lids. Try making one.

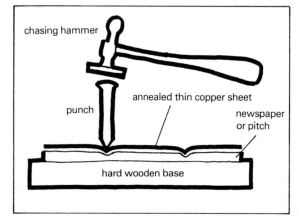

chasing hammer

punch

annealed thin copper sheet

newspaper or pitch

hard wooden base

some punch shapes

Hardening and Tempering

If you want to form one material with another your tool must be made of a harder material than the one you are shaping. In metalwork and plastics craft the tools we use are mostly made from hardened steel. Mild steel cannot be hardened very easily in a way to make it useful for tool making, so we use steels with more carbon in them. These can be hardened by changing their internal structure. We do this by heating the steel, an action which has the effect of changing the crystals which make up the metal into crystals of harder metal. If you allow the metal to cool slowly the crystals will change back to soft metal again, but if you cool the metal quickly by plunging it into cold oil, the crystals do not have time to change back into their soft form. By making tool steel red hot and then quenching it in this way you make it very hard indeed.

Unfortunately very hard steel is also very brittle, so a compromise has to be reached. If you heat the hard steel up again, but not to red heat, you will soften it slightly, which makes it tougher but still hard enough to do its job. The right temperature for this process, called **tempering**, is shown by the colour the steel goes as it is heated. For a punch the colour you want is dark brown. Once the metal has reached this colour you quench it again in oil to fix the crystals in this new state.

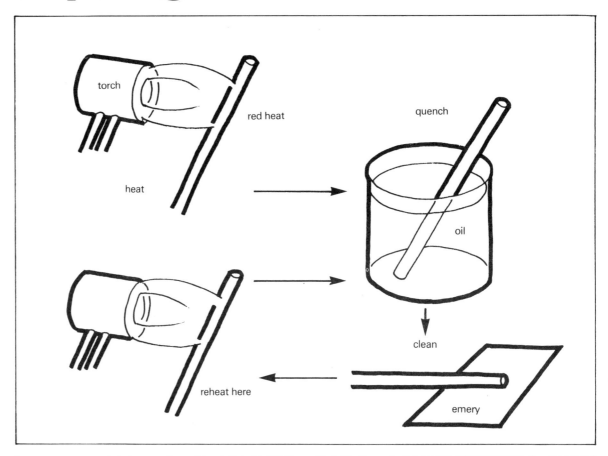

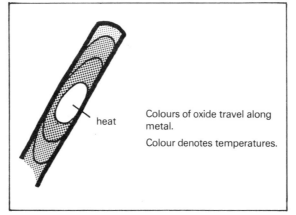

Colours of oxide travel along metal.

Colour denotes temperatures.

Tempering Chart

Colour	Temperature	Item
straw	230°C	hammers knives scribers
dark straw	245°C	drills taps dies
brown	260°C	punches
light purple	270°C	chisels screwdrivers
blue	295°C	rules saws springs

Small Chasing Punch

If you want to do some chasing on to metal sheet, or to decorate a small dish with a punched design, a small straight tool will do most of the lines you will need from straight lines to quite tight curves. The process of making the punch is very simple and involves a little forging followed by hardening and tempering.

To forge a piece of steel you have to heat the end up to red hot and then hit it with a hammer on the flat face of an anvil. This flattens the end you hit, and is very satisfying if you like making a noise!

If you start with a straight punch, you can make a small curved punch by hammering the flattened end over the tip of the pointed part of the anvil. You can also make many other shapes for use as decorative punches, or punches to make flat areas, by simply filing the end of a piece of silver steel and then hardening and tempering it.

To make your punch

You will need: A length of silver steel 5 mm diameter or hexagonal tool steel about 5 mm across flats (A.F.), a hammer, an anvil, a blow torch or forge (the blow torch is easy to use), a flat file, some oil in a tin deep enough to get the length of the punch into, emery cloth, a grindstone and an oilstone.

1   Heat the end of your rod to red heat and hammer it flat on the anvil.

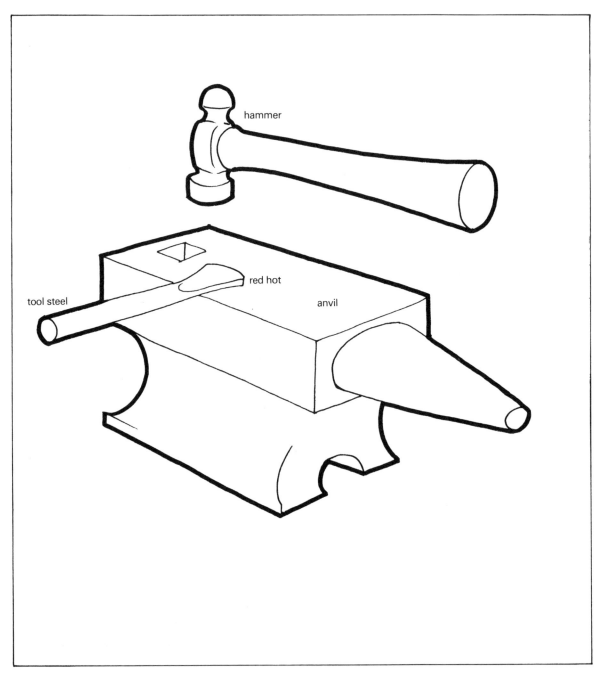

78

2   Clean up the edges and file them parallel, then file the end flat and with a slight chisel edge.

3   Heat the forged end to bright red heat and quench it immediately in oil. Do this in a well ventilated area. The oil gives off a lot of smoke.

4   Clean the end with emery cloth until it is bright. This is so that you can see the tempering colours as they move along the steel.

5   Heat the metal again but gently this time. Keep the flame small and heat the metal about 10 mm from the end. As the colours start to form take the flame away and watch the colour move along the metal. When the tip is dark brown quench it.

6   When the steel is cool cut it to about 120 mm. long and file the sawn end flat and smooth.

7   Ask your teacher to true up the edge of the punch on the grindstone and then you can finish sharpening it on a fine oilstone. Do not make it so sharp that it will cut the metal in use, but just 'soften' the tip on the oilstone.

Your punch is now ready for use.

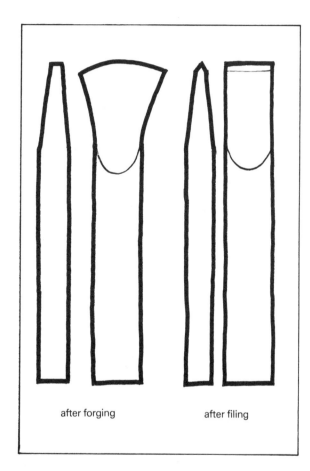

after forging   after filing

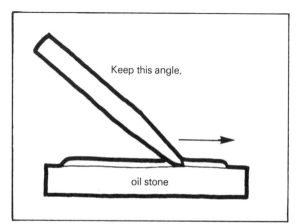

Keep this angle,

oil stone

Small Copper Pot

This little pot can be used, if you wish, as a salt pot or simply as an attractive little box for pins etc. Your design problem is to make a lid for the box out of any material you think would suit the purpose for which you will use it. You must also work out the best way, and the simplest, for the top to fit the pot. You have enough experience of the various tools and processes available to produce a suitable and sensible result. You might also consider the possibility of decorating the outside of the pot in one of the ways you have learned.

To make your pot

You will need: A piece of copper tube 25 mm diameter by 1.2–1.6 mm. wall thickness, a piece of copper sheet 27 mm square by 1.2–1.6 mm thick, some silver solder, borax flux, snips, hand file, polisher, any other tools and materials you will need to make the top.

1   True up the ends of your piece of tube by facing them in a lathe. Do not do the chuck up too tightly or you will crush the tube.

2   Clean the surface of the small piece of metal sheet with emery cloth. Put it on to a firebrick on the brazing hearth. Mix up a small amount of flux and put it on to the sheet where the tube will touch it. Dip the end of the tube into the flux and then place it on the copper sheet.

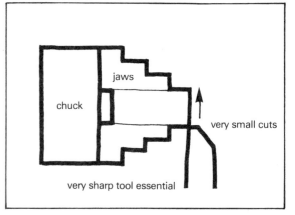

jaws

chuck

very small cuts

very sharp tool essential

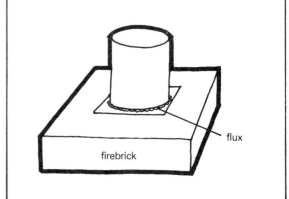

flux

firebrick

3 Cut three small pieces of silver solder (called **paillons**) and drop these down the tube so that they are arranged round the join. Make sure that they are covered with flux.

4 Heat the tube and base evenly with the blow torch from the outside until you see the solder come through the joint. Leave to cool slightly. Pickle.

5 Wash the assembly thoroughly in plenty of running water, dry it and trim the surplus metal from the base with snips. File the base flush with the sides of the tube.

6 Polish to a deep shine on the buffing machine.

7 Now it's your turn! Design and make the top. If you are making a salt pot the top must fit tightly—after all, you don't want a plateful of salt!

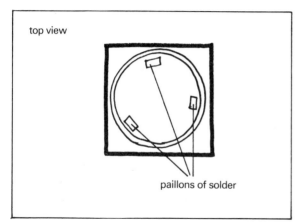

top view

paillons of solder

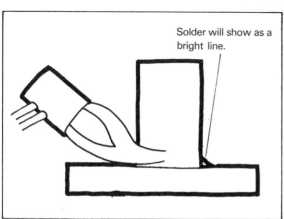

Solder will show as a bright line.

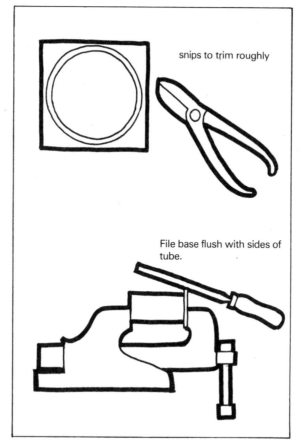

snips to trim roughly

File base flush with sides of tube.

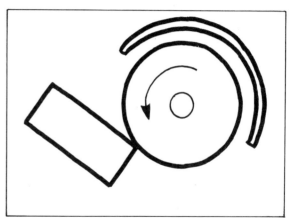

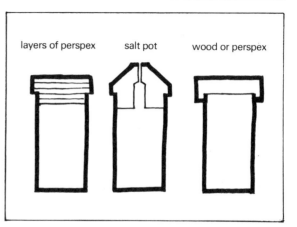

layers of perspex   salt pot   wood or perspex

Folding Metal

There are a number of jobs which require you to fold (bend) sheet metal. To do this without distorting it in any way you must support the whole length of the bend between two pieces of metal bar. If the piece you are bending is very tall you will not be able to hold it directly in the vice. To get over this problem we use **folding bars**. These tools are simply a piece of steel bar bent in the middle so that it forms a sort of clamp for the sheet to fit into. The bend is in the form of a loop, so that if the 'open' ends are held in a vice the loop acts like a spring to hold the clamp tightly shut on to the metal sheet. Now all you have to do is to tap the metal over with a hide mallet or a hammer to the angle you need.

Nowadays there are sophisticated folding machines available but they work on the same principle as folding bars.

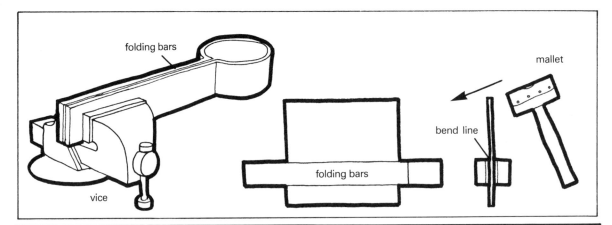

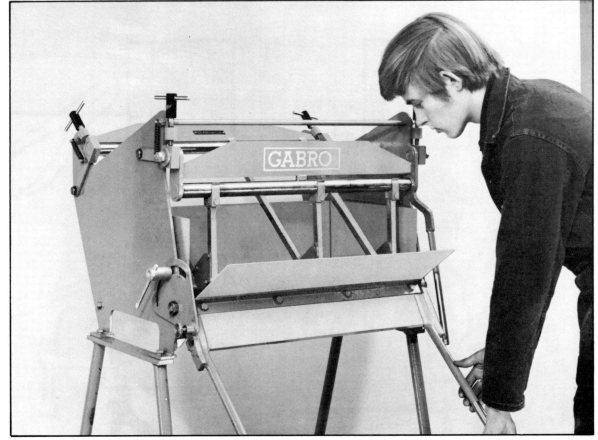

Tension File

The **tension file**, also called an **abrafile**, is a sort of saw with a completely round blade held in tension in a frame similar to a hacksaw. The advantage of such a saw is that the teeth go right round the blade so that you can saw in any direction. This means that you can cut some very complicated shapes. It also lets you cut shapes out of the middle of a piece of material by first drilling a small hole just large enough for the blade to fit through, before you fit it to the frame.

The disadvantage of this sort of saw is that the blades are extremely fragile and snap very easily.

They can be used on any type or thickness of material, and the blades are available in three grades, coarse, medium and fine, to suit your needs.

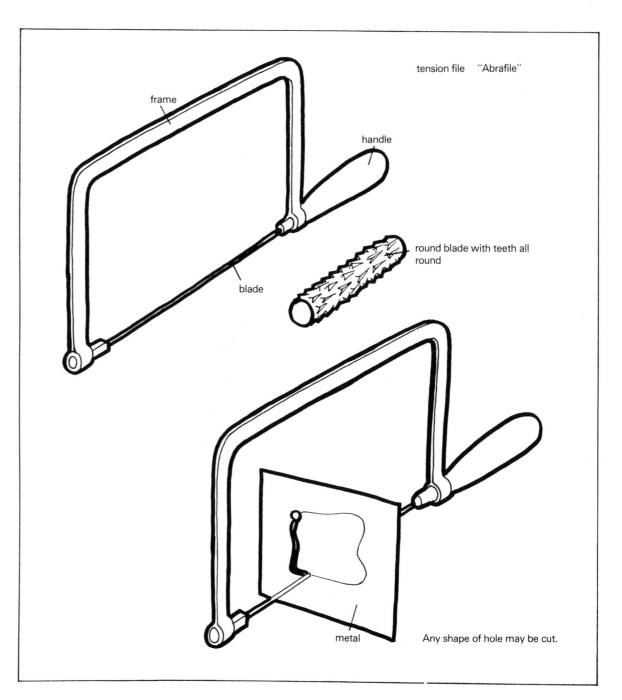

tension file   "Abrafile"

frame

handle

blade

round blade with teeth all round

metal   Any shape of hole may be cut.

Bookends

This job is one where you have to design a motif based on any of the natural, geometric or synthetic shapes you find pleasing. The bookend itself is simply a piece of bent metal sheet, the upright piece, which supports the books, being cut into the motif you have designed. As you think about this shape you must consider the problems of weight and strength of metals and books. If your design removes too much metal, especially near the bend, the bookend will collapse under the weight of the books it is supposed to be holding up. If you do not remove enough metal, the finished job may not appear very pleasing. You must strike a balance between the technical requirements and the aesthetic needs of the piece.

Your motif will be in the form of a silhouette, so it must be a form which needs no other detail than its outline in order to express itself.

To make your bookend

You will need: A piece of aluminium or mild steel sheet 250 mm by 125 mm by 2 mm, marking tools as necessary, abrafile and/or hacksaw as necessary, files as needed, folding bars, mallet or hammer.

1 Mark a line across the sheet 75 mm from one end. This is the bend line, and the large portion is the area available for your motif. Mark your design out on this piece.

2 Using the abrafile or hacksaw cut out your design. File the edges smooth.

3 Put the metal into the folding bars with the longer piece down and the bend level with the top edge of the bars. Fit the bars firmly into the vice.

4 Working gently and evenly along the bend line, hammer the metal over the bars until it forms a right angle. Take the bars out of the vice and the metal from the folding bars.

Note

If you use aluminium sheet, you should make sure that you do nothing to spoil its surface as you work it. It will be difficult to polish out all the marks afterwards. If you use steel sheet, you must protect the surface from rusting later, either by painting it or perhaps by plastic coating.

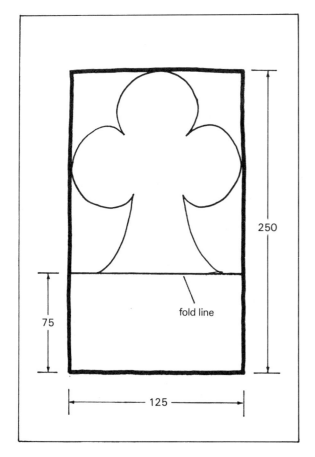

250

75

fold line

125

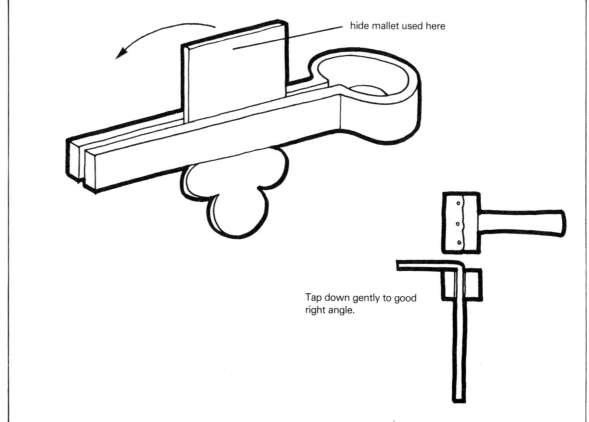

hide mallet used here

Tap down gently to good right angle.

Seaming

Seaming is a silver soldering operation which is very similar to the method you used to make up the ring base for your small dish. In this case the ring is a long one, so it has a long joint. In other words it is a tube.

The main problem with this sort of joint is to keep the two edges together while you are heating it. To do this you wire it up, as before, but with a more complicated web of iron wire. This is needed because you may need to solder a tapered tube, and wires seem to have a life of their own just when you most need them to stay in place!

To wire up a tube you first need to twist wires round the sheet itself, along the length of the tube. Three wires are usually enough. Each wire should be long enough for you to make two or three loops in it on

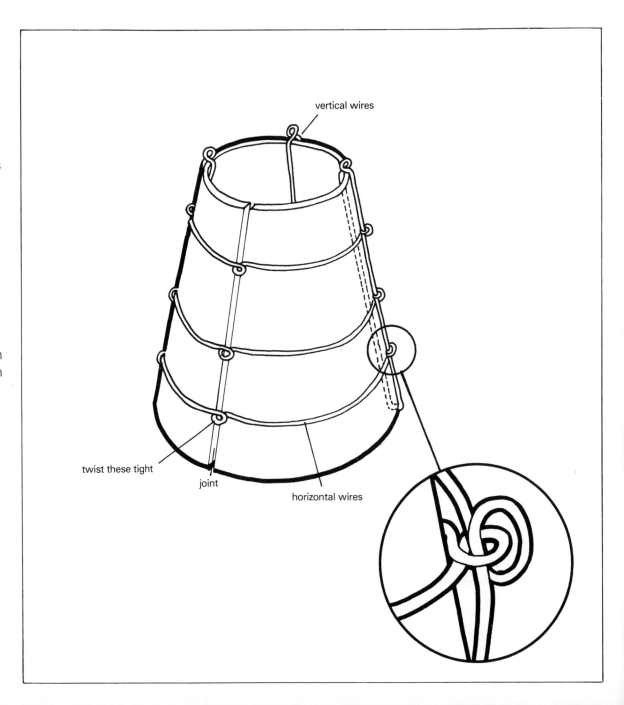

vertical wires

twist these tight

joint

horizontal wires

the outside of the tube. Other wires will now go round the tube, through these loops. You must twist these second wires round the loops in the first set so that the whole assembly is held tightly together. The ends of the second set of wires should be twisted together over the joint, pulling the edges together without touching the joint itself.

You can now flux and solder the joint in the usual way, making sure that the joint is lying horizontally on the hearth and that you apply the solder to the outside and play the flame along the inside of the tube to draw the solder through the joint.

Remove the wires before you pickle the tube or you will contaminate the acid bath with the iron wire.

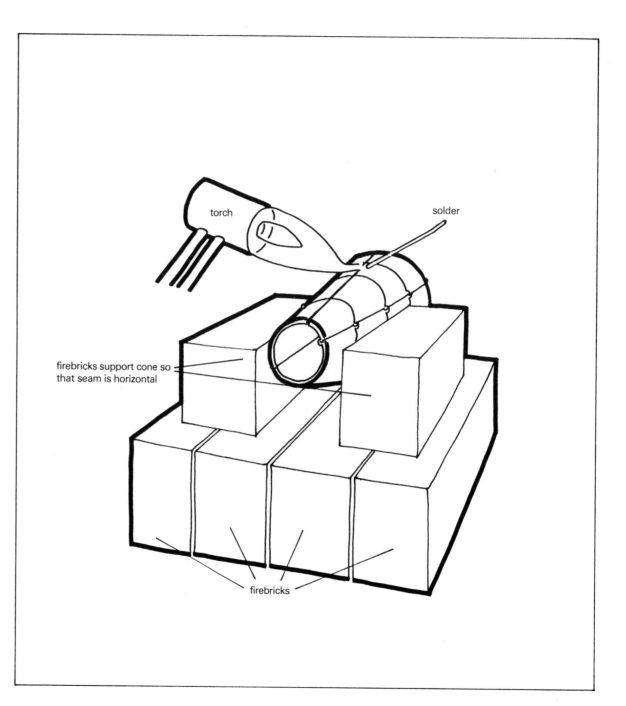

torch

solder

firebricks support cone so that seam is horizontal

firebricks

Mug

This job is similar to the small pot in its method of construction except that you have to make up the tube yourself. Also the shape of the tube is up to you; it does not have to be straight but can be tapered if you prefer. If you want to taper it you must make a 'development' of the shape. This is a drawing of the shape if you open it out flat. (See the drawing for the development of a cone.)

The other design job you have is the handle. It must be comfortable to hold, and enable you to hold the full mug safely and tip it to drink from it. You must also make it in such a way, and of suitable materials, that it can be washed up easily. The handle must also be fixed to the body of the mug without making too many holes that will be difficult to seal. If it leaks you will have your drinks running down your sleeve!

To make your mug

You will need: 1.2 mm thick gilding metal sheet, materials for your handle, all the materials and tools for hammering and soldering with silver solder.

1 Draw out the development of the body of the mug on a piece of card. Cut it out and transfer the design on to a piece of metal sheet.

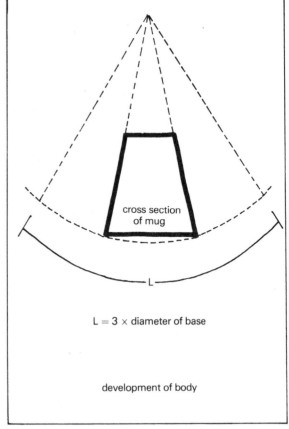

cross section of mug

L

L = 3 × diameter of base

development of body

2　Cut out the development and file the edges smooth. Using the hide mallet, form the sheet round a funnel stake to make your tube.

3　Make sure that the edges of the joint will meet along their entire length, and wire it up as described in the section on seaming.

4　Solder the seam using hard silver solder.

5　True up the bottom edge on a piece of emery cloth, and cut a piece of metal sheet into a circle a little bigger than the bottom. Wire these together.

6　Solder the bottom to the body, using medium grade silver solder.

7　Trim the bottom and true up the top. Clean up the joints and polish the mug all over. Be sure to clean the inside very well, as this will contain what that you are going to drink.

8　Make up your handle to your design and fix it to the body. If you are soldering the two pieces together, do it near the seam, but use easy-flo solder with great care so that you do not open the seam up.

9　Polish again.

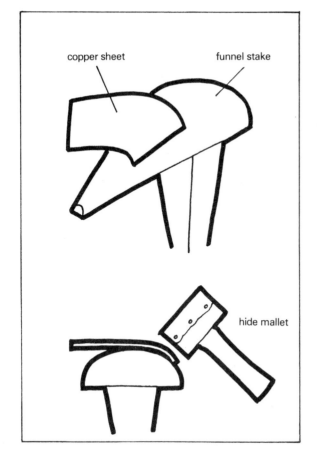

copper sheet

funnel stake

hide mallet

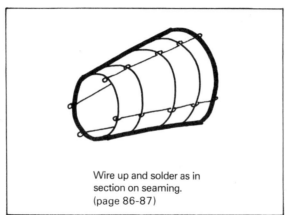

Wire up and solder as in section on seaming. (page 86-87)

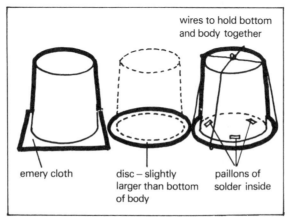

wires to hold bottom and body together

emery cloth

disc – slightly larger than bottom of body

paillons of solder inside

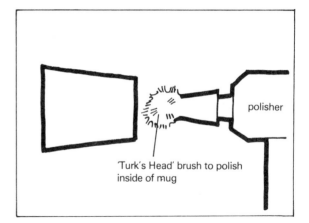

polisher

'Turk's Head' brush to polish inside of mug

metal handle soldered over seam to 'hide' it

Salad Servers

For this job you are going to design a pair of salad servers which you will make using a former to press heated Acrylic sheet into shape. There are also two possible forms this article can take. One is separate 'spoon and fork' servers, and the other is a sort of 'tong' arrangement in which the spoon and fork are joined by a springy piece of material. By using a long piece of Acrylic sheet and bending it in the middle, you can make the second type in one piece. The old 'spoon and fork' salad servers are not necessarily the best shape for the job, so exercise your design talents on that problem as well as the general layout of the job.

To make the formers you will need to use a piece of wood cut to the contours of your servers. To do this you will either use a coping saw or bow saw or, if you have access to one, you can speed the whole job up by using a band saw.

To make your salad servers

You will need: 3 mm thick acrylic sheet, 600 mm long by 50 mm wide, saws, files, emery cloth, polisher, former and oven.

1   Draw out the shape of your servers on the paper covering the acrylic sheet. Cut them out and file, emery cloth and polish the edges.
2   Make up your former from softwood or hardwood. Old furniture is a very good source of such timber. To save on the number of formers a class will need you

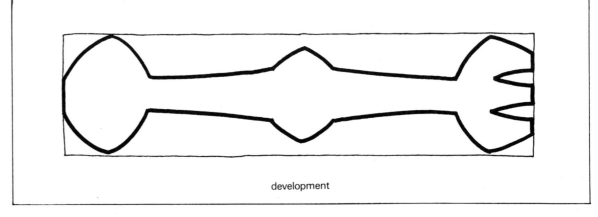

development

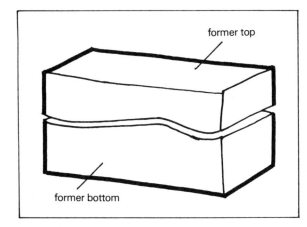

former top

former bottom

could work in groups of three or four to
make and share a former. The surfaces of
the former which will be in contact with
the plastic sheet must be sanded down
perfectly smooth.

3   Remove the paper from the acrylic
sheet and place it in an oven set at 150°C
until it is soft and floppy. Place it
accurately on one half of the former and
press the other half on top, holding the
two halves together until the plastic has
set into shape. Use a pair of heat resistant
gloves to handle the plastic.

If you are making the bent tongs heat only
one end at a time in the oven. Reheating
acrylic sheet makes it return to its original
flat form.

4   If you are making the tongs, wear
heat-resistant gloves to hold the area to be
bent over an electric hotplate until it is
soft, and then bend it by hand or over a
dowel former to the shape you want. Cool
it under the tap to set it.

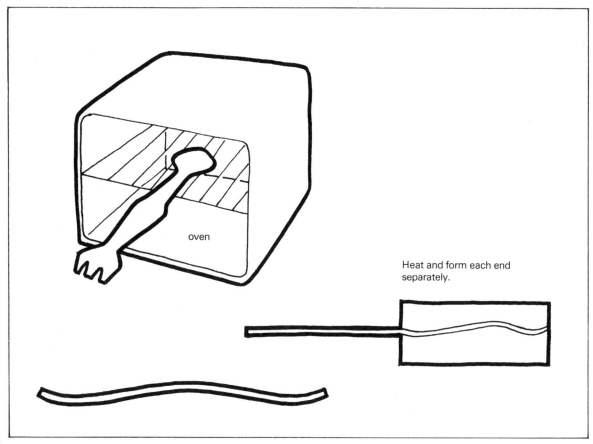

oven

Heat and form each end
separately.

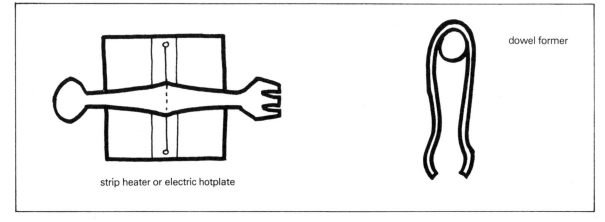

strip heater or electric hotplate

dowel former

Cassette or Spice Jar Rack

Here is a job to exercise all your design talents and technological knowledge and skill. It is again in the form of a problem to be solved by you, using all the experience you have acquired by following this course. You have to choose materials and processes and explain, in writing, why you have chosen them. By combining your explanation with your sketches and drawings of the job, you are following the design process that is used by the professional designers.

Instructions

1 Design and make a rack, suitable for use in a kitchen, to hold six small jars of herbs or spices. It must be possible to see and read the labels; and the bottles must be securely held to avoid the possibility of accidental breakage, but at the same time easy to remove and replace while making a meal. This may mean that the bottles will be used by someone with greasy hands, so the bottles and the rack must be easy to clean. The material the rack is made from must be able to stand up to the atmosphere of a kitchen.

or

2 Design and make a rack, suitable for use in a living room or bedroom, to hold twelve cassette tapes. The tapes must be easy to identify, and easy to take out and put back but at the same time held safely in place so that they cannot fall out and get damaged. You may need to provide some form of extra lighting because the rack may be used in conditions of near darkness!

Group Projects

There are many projects that are too complicated and involved for you to carry out by yourself, but which are very interesting experiments for a group of you, working together, to have a go at. You will have problems of design and method to consider in these projects and you will also have to use the school library for information.

The way in which you tackle these projects is up to the group to decide but several possible approaches are given for you to consider.

1   Water power

Problem

Lift a 1 kg weight from the floor to the top of the work bench using water as your source of power.

Suggested approaches

a)   Water wheels or turbines driven from a tank of water (or the tap). Gears or pulleys will give you a mechanical advantage so that a simple apparatus can lift quite a considerable load.

b)   Hydraulic power, using a sufficient 'head' of water to raise a jack of some sort.

c)   Steam power, by heating the water to provide energy in the form of steam to drive engines or turbines.

2 Structural support

Problem

Using materials of a maximum thickness of 3 mm support a 1 kg weight over the centre of a gap 500 mm wide.

Suggested approaches

This problem is one which depends on the relative strengths of different materials, different sections of materials and different methods of construction.

a)   Look at any bridge to see what sort of girders are used. The shape is important.

b)   Look at the relative strengths of materials of differently shaped cross-sections. Tubes are stronger for some jobs than solid material of the same size!

c)   By seeing how the weight has to be carried at the ends of the gap, you might make up a platform, or a series of web-like girders, or even a suspension type of construction.

There is no requirement for there to be solid material all the way across the gap!

Group Projects

3 Motive Power Comparison

Problem

There are many different forms of motive power used in transporting people around towns. All are one way or another based on 'fossil fuels', that is oil and coal, for their basic energy needs. Find out the most economical form of power to use for driving a small city transport such as a commuter car.

Suggested approaches

Compare the relative merits as power units of electric motors, external combustion engines (steam or hot air engines for example) and internal combustion engines (petrol and diesel).

a)   Make small engines of each type and see how much power they give.
b)   Compare the cost of making each engine in terms of materials, technology needed and time needed.
c)   See how much each type of engine costs in fuel to produce the same amount of 'travel'. You will have to invent some suitable laboratory experiment.
d)   Compare the types of engine for their ease of maintenance.
e)   Investigate the 'environmental damage' of the various types of engine.

An alternative project on the same lines could be to investigate the most efficient way to transport bulk cargoes of freight inside the country. The areas you can investigate are the relative costs in terms of energy resources and environmental impact, at both a national and personal level, of road, rail, air and water transport. The relevant questions are similar to those you must ask about the different sorts of engine for urban transport.